NO FEAR SHAKESPEARE

NO FEAR SHAKESPEARE

Antony and Cleopatra

As You Like It

The Comedy of Errors

Coriolanus

Hamlet

Henry IV, Parts One and Two

Henry V

Julius Caesar

King Lear

Macbeth

Measure for Measure

The Merchant of Venice

A Midsummer Night's Dream

Much Ado About Nothing

Othello

Richard III

Romeo and Juliet

Sonnets

The Taming of the Shrew

The Tempest

Twelfth Night

Two Gentlemen of Verona

Winter's Tale

NO FEAR SHAKESPEARE

RICHARD II

*sparknotes

ISBN 978-1-4549-2805-8

Distributed in Canada by Sterling Publishing Co., Inc.
c/o Canadian Manda Group, 664 Annette Street
Toronto, Ontario M6S 2C8, Canada
Distributed in the United Kingdom by GMC Distribution Services
Castle Place, 166 High Street, Lewes, East Sussex BN7 1XU, England
Distributed in Australia by NewSouth Books
45 Beach Street, Coogee, NSW 2034, Australia

For information about custom editions, special sales, and premium
and corporate purchases, please contact Sterling Special Sales at
800-805-5489 or specialsales@sterlingpublishing.com.

Manufactured in the United States of America

Lot #:
2 4 6 8 10 9 7 5 3 1

10/17

sterlingpublishing.com
sparknotes.com

Cover and title page illustration by Richard Amari.

There's matter in these sighs, these profound heaves.
You must translate: 'tis fit we understand them.

(*Hamlet,* 4.1.1–2)

FEAR NOT.

Have you ever found yourself looking at a Shakespeare play, then down at the footnotes, then back up at the play, and still not understanding? You know what the individual words mean, but they don't add up. SparkNotes' *No Fear Shakespeare* will help you break through all that. Put the pieces together with our easy-to-read translations. Soon you'll be reading Shakespeare's own words fearlessly—and actually enjoying it.

No Fear Shakespeare puts Shakespeare's language side-by-side with a facing-page translation into modern English—the kind of English people actually speak today. When Shakespeare's words make your head spin, our translation will help you sort out what's happening, who's saying what, and why.

RICHARD II

CHARACTERS

King Richard II—The King of England when the play begins. Stately and poetic, though immature, King Richard enjoys the trappings of kingship and has an extraordinary flair for poetic language. He is overthrown by his cousin, Henry Bolingbroke, and eventually assassinated in the remote castle of Pomfret.

Henry Bolingbroke (also known as Harry)—King Richard's cousin, Duke of Hereford, and the son of Richard's uncle, John of Gaunt. He is less poetic but far more pragmatic and capable than his cousin. He returns from his banishment abroad and stages a revolution against Richard II. He is eventually crowned King Henry IV.

John of Gaunt—An important nobleman and Richard's uncle. John of Gaunt is referred to as either "Gaunt" or "Lancaster." He dies of old age after the banishment of his son Henry, but not before delivering a withering curse on Richard.

Duke of York—Richard's uncle and a brother of John of Gaunt and of the late Thomas of Gloucester. King Richard makes York Lord Governor of England, but Bolingbroke convinces him to defect and join his rebel army. A traditionalist who is loyally devoted to the crown, he is deeply upset by any kind of treason against the crown.

Duke of Aumerle—The son of Edmund, Duke of York. He remains loyal to his cousin Richard throughout the war and, after Richard's deposition, is involved in a failed scheme against the life of the newly crowned King Henry IV. Also called "Rutland" late in the play, since he is the Earl of Rutland.

Thomas Mowbray—A nobleman whom Henry Bolingbroke accuses, early in the play, of treason against the state and of complicity in the earlier death of Richard's uncle Thomas, Duke of Gloucester. Mowbray is banished at the same time as Bolingbroke and dies in exile. Also called "Norfolk," as he is the Duke of Norfolk.

Bushy, Bagot, and Green—Richard's friends and loyal backers in the court. Bushy and Green are trapped by Bolingbroke and executed. Bagot, also captured, becomes an informer and apparently survives the play.

Northumberland, Lord Ross, and Lord Willoughby—Noblemen who join Bolingbroke's rebel army early to fight against King Richard. Northumberland (occasionally called "Percy") is the father of young Henry Percy (also called "Percy").

Henry Percy—Northumberland's son. He joins Bolingbroke's rebels along with his father.

Duchess of York—The wife of the Duke of York and mother of the Duke of Aumerle. She goes before King Henry to plead for her son's life.

Duchess of Gloucester—The aged widow of the late Thomas of Gloucester, and the sister-in-law of John of Gaunt and the Duke of York. She resides in a house at Plashy and dies offstage during the play.

Queen Isabel—King Richard's wife. She was born into the French royal family and flees to France when Richard is deposed.

Thomas Percy, Earl of Worcester—The lord steward of the king's household. Thomas Percy is also the brother of Henry Percy, Earl of Northumberland, and thus the uncle of young Henry Percy. When Northumberland is declared a traitor, Worcester defects to Bolingbroke, taking the servants of the king's house with him. He does not appear in the play but other characters refer to him often.

Lord Berkeley—The ruler of Berkeley Castle in Gloucestershire, where York's army meets Bolingbroke's army. Berkeley is loyal to King Richard.

Lord Salisbury—A lord loyal to King Richard. He is eventually beheaded for his part in the conspiracy against the life of the newly crowned King Henry IV.

Bishop of Carlisle—A clergyman loyal to Richard. He is arrested for speaking out against Bolingbroke's usurpation of the throne. He is later indicted in the conspiracy against King Henry's life, but the king pardons him and sends him away from the court.

Sir Stephen Scroop—A nobleman loyal to Richard. He brings Richard the bad news of Bolingbroke's invasion when Richard returns from Ireland.

Abbot of Westminster—A clergyman loyal to Richard. He is beheaded for his participation in the conspiracy against King Henry's life.

Exton—A nobleman who assassinates the former King Richard in Pomfret Castle, believing himself to be acting under King Henry's orders

Lord Fitzwater—A minor lord.

NO FEAR SHAKESPEARE

RICHARD II

ACT ONE
SCENE 1

London, King Richard II's palace. Enter **KING RICHARD II**,
JOHN OF GAUNT, *with other Nobles and Attendants*

KING RICHARD II

Old John of Gaunt, time-honor'd Lancaster,
Hast thou, according to thy oath and band,
Brought hither Henry Hereford thy bold son,
Here to make good the boisterous late appeal,
5   Which then our leisure would not let us hear,
Against the Duke of Norfolk, Thomas Mowbray?

JOHN OF GAUNT

I have, my liege.

KING RICHARD II

Tell me, moreover, hast thou sounded him,
If he appeal the duke on ancient malice;
10   Or worthily, as a good subject should,
On some known ground of treachery in him?

JOHN OF GAUNT

As near as I could sift him on that argument,
On some apparent danger seen in him
Aim'd at your highness, no inveterate malice.

KING RICHARD II

15   Then call them to our presence; face to face,
And frowning brow to brow, ourselves will hear
The accuser and the accused freely speak.
High-stomach'd are they both, and full of ire,
In rage deaf as the sea, hasty as fire.

Enter **HENRY BOLINGBROKE** *and* **THOMAS MOWBRAY**

ACT ONE
SCENE 1

London. King Richard II's palace KING RICHARD II, JOHN OF
GAUNT, *and other nobles and attendants enter.*

KING RICHARD II

Old John of Gaunt, did you do as you promised and
bring your brave son Henry here? I'd like to hear the
violent accusation he wanted to make against the Duke of
Norfolk, Thomas Mowbray, which I didn't have time to
deal with earlier.

JOHN OF GAUNT

I've brought him, my lord.

KING RICHARD II

Have you asked him if the source of his complaint is
an old feud or if he knows of some treason the duke
has committed?

JOHN OF GAUNT

As far as I could tell, it's not personal malice. My son
believes that the duke means to harm you in some way.

KING RICHARD II

Then call them both in to see me. I want to hear in person
what each has to say. They're both so proud and full of
anger that they act recklessly and don't listen to reason.

HENRY BOLINGBROKE *and* **THOMAS MOWBRAY** *enter.*

HENRY BOLINGBROKE

20   Many years of happy days befall
      My gracious sovereign, my most loving liege!

THOMAS MOWBRAY

      Each day still better other's happiness;
      Until the heavens, envying earth's good hap,
      Add an immortal title to your crown!

KING RICHARD II

25   We thank you both. Yet one but flatters us,
      As well appeareth by the cause you come:
      Namely to appeal each other of high treason.
      Cousin of Hereford, what dost thou object
      Against the Duke of Norfolk, Thomas Mowbray?

HENRY BOLINGBROKE

30   First— heaven be the record to my speech!—
      In the devotion of a subject's love,
      Tend'ring the precious safety of my prince,
      And free from other misbegotten hate,
      Come I appellant to this princely presence.
35   Now, Thomas Mowbray, do I turn to thee,
      And mark my greeting well; for what I speak
      My body shall make good upon this earth,
      Or my divine soul answer it in heaven.
      Thou art a traitor and a miscreant,
40   Too good to be so and too bad to live,
      Since the more fair and crystal is the sky,
      The uglier seem the clouds that in it fly.
      Once more, the more to aggravate the note,
      With a foul traitor's name stuff I thy throat;
45   And wish, so please my sovereign, ere I move,
      What my tongue speaks my right-drawn sword may prove.

THOMAS MOWBRAY

      Let not my cold words here accuse my zeal.
      'Tis not the trial of a woman's war,
      The bitter clamor of two eager tongues,
50   Can arbitrate this cause betwixt us twain.

HENRY BOLINGBROKE

> May you have many years of happiness, my gracious and
> loving lord.

THOMAS MOWBRAY

> May each day be happier than the last, and heaven give
> you immortality!

KING RICHARD II

> Thank you both. But I know one of you isn't sincere,
> since each of you accuses the other of treason against me.
> Henry of Hereford, what do you have to say against the
> Duke of Norfolk, Thomas Mowbray?

HENRY BOLINGBROKE

> First, may heaven be my witness! I've come here as an
> accuser because I am a devoted subject who cares for the
> safety of my prince, not because of any other prejudice
> against the duke. Now, Thomas Mowbray, I will turn
> to you. Pay attention to this. I will prove that what I am
> about to say is true, either with my body here on earth or
> with my immortal soul in heaven. You are a traitor and a
> villain, born into too good a family to be so and too bad
> to live. The more beautiful the sky, the uglier the clouds
> look. Once more, to emphasize my accusation, I call
> you a traitor. And with my king's permission, I'd like to
> follow what I say with my sword.

THOMAS MOWBRAY

> Don't let my calm words cast doubt on my loyalty. I
> know that angry words will not settle this argument, so
> I'll try to keep myself under control. But I can't be so
> calm as to not say anything in my own defense. First, my

The blood is hot that must be cool'd for this.
Yet can I not of such tame patience boast
As to be hush'd and nought at all to say.
First, the fair reverence of your highness curbs me
55 From giving reins and spurs to my free speech,
Which else would post until it had return'd
These terms of treason doubled down his throat.
Setting aside his high blood's royalty,
And let him be no kinsman to my liege,
60 I do defy him, and I spit at him.
Call him a slanderous coward and a villain,
Which to maintain I would allow him odds,
And meet him, were I tied to run afoot
Even to the frozen ridges of the Alps,
65 Or any other ground inhabitable,
Where ever Englishman durst set his foot.
Meantime let this defend my loyalty—
By all my hopes, most falsely doth he lie.

HENRY BOLINGBROKE

Pale trembling coward, there I throw my gage,
70 Disclaiming here the kindred of the king,
And lay aside my high blood's royalty,
Which fear, not reverence, makes thee to except.
If guilty dread have left thee so much strength
As to take up mine honor's pawn, then stoop.
75 By that and all the rites of knighthood else,
Will I make good against thee, arm to arm,
What I have spoke, or thou canst worse devise.

THOMAS MOWBRAY

I take it up. And by that sword I swear
Which gently laid my knighthood on my shoulder,
80 I'll answer thee in any fair degree,
Or chivalrous design of knightly trial;
And when I mount, alive may I not light,
If I be traitor or unjustly fight!

respect for you, my king, prevents me from saying what I want and throwing those charges of treason right back at Bolingbroke. I defy him and spit on him as if he weren't your relative, my lord. He's a trash-talking coward and a villain, and I'd back up those charges in a duel, even if I gave him an advantage by handicapping myself. For now, I've defended my loyalty and made it known that he lies.

HENRY BOLINGBROKE

You pale coward. There I'll throw my glove in challenge to you and set aside my relationship to the king and my royal blood. It's fear—not respect for the king's bloodline—that keeps you quiet. If your guilt has given you the guts to accept my challenge, then pick up my glove. I'll show your cowardice and treason by defeating you in knightly combat.

THOMAS MOWBRAY

I'll take that challenge. And I promise, by my knighthood, that I'll fight you fairly in whatever contest you wish. And when I mount my horse, let me not dismount alive if I'm a traitor or if I cheat in any way!

KING RICHARD II

      What doth our cousin lay to Mowbray's charge?
85   It must be great that can inherit us
      So much as of a thought of ill in him.

HENRY BOLINGBROKE

      Look, what I speak, my life shall prove it true;
      That Mowbray hath received eight thousand nobles
      In name of lendings for your highness' soldiers,
90   The which he hath detain'd for lewd employments,
      Like a false traitor and injurious villain.
      Besides I say and will in battle prove,
      Or here or elsewhere to the furthest verge
      That ever was survey'd by English eye,
95   That all the treasons for these eighteen years
      Complotted and contrived in this land
      Fetch from false Mowbray their first head and spring.
      Further I say and further will maintain
      Upon his bad life to make all this good,
100   That he did plot the Duke of Gloucester's death,
      Suggest his soon-believing adversaries,
      And consequently, like a traitor coward,
      Sluiced out his innocent soul through streams of blood:
      Which blood, like sacrificing Abel's, cries,
105   Even from the tongueless caverns of the earth,
      To me for justice and rough chastisement.
      And, by the glorious worth of my descent,
      This arm shall do it, or this life be spent.

KING RICHARD II

      How high a pitch his resolution soars!
110   Thomas of Norfolk, what say'st thou to this?

THOMAS MOWBRAY

      O, let my sovereign turn away his face
      And bid his ears a little while be deaf,
      Till I have told this slander of his blood
      How God and good men hate so foul a liar.

KING RICHARD II

What do you accuse Mowbray of, my cousin? It must be
something terrible if it's going to make me think badly of
him in any way.

HENRY BOLINGBROKE

I'll prove with my life that what I say is true.
Mowbray has received eight thousand gold coins
that he was supposed to pay to your soldiers as
advances on their wages. But he's used the money
improperly, just as a traitor and harmful villain
would. Even more, I declare and will prove in battle
that all treasonous plots over the past eighteen years
originated with Mowbray. And further, I know
that he caused the Duke of Gloucester's death by
encouraging the duke's easily influenced enemies, as
any coward would, to slay the innocent duke.
The duke was murdered like **Abel**, and his blood
demands that I seek revenge and justice. By my own
good name, I'll inflict that justice on Mowbray or die
trying.

*Refers to the
biblical story of
Cain and Abel, in
which Cain kills
his brother Abel
out of jealousy.*

KING RICHARD II

He is so determined! Thomas, how do you respond?

THOMAS MOWBRAY

I wish you would turn away and not listen till I've told
this fellow, who disgraces his bloodline, how much God
and good men hate liars like him.

KING RICHARD II

115 Mowbray, impartial are our eyes and ears.
Were he my brother, nay, my kingdom's heir,
As he is but my father's brother's son,
Now, by my scepter's awe, I make a vow:
Such neighbor nearness to our sacred blood
120 Should nothing privilege him, nor partialize
The unstooping firmness of my upright soul.
He is our subject, Mowbray; so art thou.
Free speech and fearless I to thee allow.

THOMAS MOWBRAY

Then, Bolingbroke, as low as to thy heart,
125 Through the false passage of thy throat, thou liest.
Three parts of that receipt I had for Calais
Disbursed I duly to his highness' soldiers;
The other part reserved I by consent,
For that my sovereign liege was in my debt
130 Upon remainder of a dear account,
Since last I went to France to fetch his queen.
Now swallow down that lie. For Gloucester's death,
I slew him not, but to my own disgrace
Neglected my sworn duty in that case.
135 For you, my noble Lord of Lancaster,
The honorable father to my foe
Once did I lay an ambush for your life,
A trespass that doth vex my grieved soul.
But ere I last received the sacrament
140 I did confess it, and exactly begg'd
Your grace's pardon, and I hope I had it.
This is my fault. As for the rest appeall'd,
It issues from the rancor of a villain,
A recreant and most degenerate traitor
145 Which in myself I boldly will defend;
And interchangeably hurl down my gage
Upon this overweening traitor's foot,
To prove myself a loyal gentleman

KING RICHARD II

Mowbray, my eyes and ears are impartial, even if he were my brother, or even my heir, rather than just my cousin. I vow on my scepter that his relation to me doesn't give him any advantage or prejudice me in his favor. He's my subject, Mowbray, and so are you, so speak freely and without fear.

THOMAS MOWBRAY

Then, Bolingbroke, you lie from your heart up through your false throat. I gave three quarters of the money I received to the king's soldiers. The other quarter I had permission to keep, because I was owed the money for my service in going to fetch the queen from France. Now take back your lie. As for Gloucester, I didn't kill him, but I admit I disgracefully neglected my duty. I once laid in wait to kill you, my noble lord of Lancaster, the father of my enemy. It was a terrible sin and it troubles me greatly. But I confessed it already and specifically begged your pardon, and I hoped you had forgiven me. That is my fault. As for the rest of the charges, they come from a villain's evil nature, and I'll defend myself against this faithless and cowardly traitor. I'll throw my glove down onto this arrogant traitor's foot, and I'll show that I'm loyal even compared to this member of the royal bloodline. I therefore pray that your highness will assign a day for our duel soon.

Even in the best blood chamber'd in his bosom.
150 In haste whereof, most heartily I pray
Your highness to assign our trial day.

KING RICHARD II

Wrath-kindled gentlemen, be ruled by me.
Let's purge this choler without letting blood.
This we prescribe, though no physician.
155 Deep malice makes too deep incision;
Forget, forgive; conclude and be agreed.
Our doctors say this is no month to bleed.
Good uncle, let this end where it begun;
We'll calm the Duke of Norfolk, you your son.

JOHN OF GAUNT

160 To be a make-peace shall become my age:
Throw down, my son, the Duke of Norfolk's gage.

KING RICHARD II

And, Norfolk, throw down his.

JOHN OF GAUNT

When, Harry, when?
Obedience bids I should not bid again.

KING RICHARD II

165 Norfolk, throw down, we bid; there is no boot.

THOMAS MOWBRAY

Myself I throw, dread sovereign, at thy foot.
My life thou shalt command, but not my shame.
The one my duty owes, but my fair name,
Despite of death that lives upon my grave,
170 To dark dishonor's use thou shalt not have.
I am disgraced, impeach'd, and baffled here,
Pierced to the soul with slander's venom'd spear,
The which no balm can cure but his heart-blood
Which breathed this poison.

KING RICHARD II

175 Rage must be withstood.
Give me his gage: lions make leopards tame.

KING RICHARD II

Obey what I say, my hot-headed gentlemen. Let's settle this feud without violence. Such fierce anger causes too great an injury. Forget it and forgive each other. Come to terms and agree to put this to an end. The astrologers have said that this is no month to shed blood. Good uncle, let's end this now. I'll calm down the Duke of Norfolk. You calm down your son.

JOHN OF GAUNT

For someone my age it is appropriate to make peace. My son, throw down the Duke of Norfolk's glove.

KING RICHARD II

And Norfolk, throw down his.

JOHN OF GAUNT

Come on, Henry, when are you going to do it? I shouldn't have to ask you again.

KING RICHARD II

Throw it down, Norfolk, I'm telling you. There is no advantage in refusing.

THOMAS MOWBRAY

I'll throw myself at your feet, most revered king. You may command my life, but not my shame. I owe you my life out of duty, but I cannot, even under pain of death, let you order this dishonor of my good reputation. I am accused and disgraced publicly here, pierced by the venom of slander. The only thing that will ease that pain is to kill the man who uttered these poisonous words.

KING RICHARD II

Such rage should be resisted. Give me his glove. I, as king, will tame these lesser nobles.

THOMAS MOWBRAY
     Yea, but not change his spots. Take but my shame.
     And I resign my gage. My dear dear lord,
     The purest treasure mortal times afford
180   Is spotless reputation; that away,
     Men are but gilded loam or painted clay.
     A jewel in a ten-times-barr'd-up chest
     Is a bold spirit in a loyal breast.
     Mine honor is my life; both grow in one.
185   Take honor from me, and my life is done.
     Then, dear my liege, mine honor let me try;
     In that I live and for that will I die.

KING RICHARD II
     Cousin, throw up your gage. Do you begin.

HENRY BOLINGBROKE
     O, God defend my soul from such deep sin!
190   Shall I seem crestfallen in my father's sight?
     Or with pale beggar-fear impeach my height
     Before this outdared dastard? Ere my tongue
     Shall wound my honor with such feeble wrong,
     Or sound so base a parle, my teeth shall tear
195   The slavish motive of recanting fear,
     And spit it bleeding in his high disgrace,
     Where shame doth harbor, even in Mowbray's face.

Exit JOHN OF GAUNT

KING RICHARD II
     We were not born to sue, but to command;
     Which since we cannot do to make you friends,
200   Be ready, as your lives shall answer it,
     At Coventry, upon Saint Lambert's day.
     There shall your swords and lances arbitrate
     The swelling difference of your settled hate.
     Since we cannot atone you, we shall see
205   Justice design the victor's chivalry.
     Lord marshal, command our officers at arms
     Be ready to direct these home alarms.

Exeunt

THOMAS MOWBRAY

> Yes, but you won't take away the stain of these charges. If you'll clear my name, I'll give up my glove. My dear, dear lord, the greatest treasure in our earthly lives is to have a good reputation. Without that, men are nothing. To have a brave spirit is as valuable as a well-guarded jewel. My honor is my life. One is inseparable from the other. Take my honor, and my life is over. So, my lord, let me prove my honor, since I live for it and I will die for it.

KING RICHARD II

> Cousin, take up your glove. Be the one to start.

HENRY BOLINGBROKE

> Oh, God, keep me from such a terrible sin! Should I appear humbled in front of my father? Or discredit my rank out of fear before this terrified coward? Before I'd let my tongue utter such lies against my honor or make such a false truce, I'd rip it apart with my teeth and spit it into Mowbray's shameful face.

> **JOHN OF GAUNT** *exits.*

KING RICHARD II

> I was born to command, not to beg. But since I can't order you to be friends, be ready to settle this feud with your lives at Coventry on **Saint Lambert's day**. Then you can let your weapons resolve this hatred, since I can't bring you to terms. Justice will be on the side of the winner. Lord marshal, tell my officers to be ready to control these domestic disturbances.

September 17.

> *Everyone exits.*

ACT 1, SCENE 2

The Duke of Lancaster's palace. Enter JOHN OF GAUNT *with* DUCHESS

JOHN OF GAUNT

Alas, the part I had in Woodstock's blood
Doth more solicit me than your exclaims,
To stir against the butchers of his life!
But since correction lieth in those hands
5   Which made the fault that we cannot correct,
Put we our quarrel to the will of heaven;
Who, when they see the hours ripe on earth,
Will rain hot vengeance on offenders' heads.

DUCHESS

Finds brotherhood in thee no sharper spur?
10   Hath love in thy old blood no living fire?
Edward's seven sons, whereof thyself art one,
Were as seven vials of his sacred blood,
Or seven fair branches springing from one root.
Some of those seven are dried by nature's course,
15   Some of those branches by the Destinies cut;
But Thomas, my dear lord, my life, my Gloucester,
One vial full of Edward's sacred blood,
One flourishing branch of his most royal root,
Is crack'd, and all the precious liquor spilt,
20   Is hack'd down, and his summer leaves all faded,
By envy's hand and murder's bloody axe.
Ah, Gaunt, his blood was thine! That bed, that womb,
That metal, that self-mold, that fashion'd thee
Made him a man; and though thou livest and breathest,
25   Yet art thou slain in him. Thou dost consent
In some large measure to thy father's death,
In that thou seest thy wretched brother die,
Who was the model of thy father's life.
Call it not patience, Gaunt; it is despair.

ACT 1, SCENE 2

The Duke of Lancaster's palace. JOHN OF GAUNT *and the* DUCHESS OF GLOUCESTER *enter.*

JOHN OF GAUNT

Even more than your uproar, it's the fact that the Duke of Gloucester was my brother that makes me want to act against his murderers. But since it was Richard who was responsible for the murder in the first place, and also controls how it will be avenged, I'll have to trust in the will of heaven to bring justice to my brother's killers.

DUCHESS OF GLOUCESTER

Don't you feel compelled to do more since he was your brother? Is there no passion in your love for him? Your father, **Edward**, treasured you and your six brothers. Some of you died natural deaths and some of your lives were cut short. But Thomas, whom I loved and who was one of Edward's precious sons, is dead, killed by people who hated him. Oh, Gaunt, he was your own blood! The same mother and father who made you made him, and though you live and breathe, a part of you died with him. And because your father was the model for him, by watching him die you have in a sense consented to see your father die. You aren't being patient. You're giving up. In allowing your brother to be murdered, you have shown how you yourself might be killed. What we might call patience in common men is simply cowardice in noble men. What else can I say? The best way to protect your own life is to get revenge for Gloucester's death.

> Edward III, who was king of England from 1327 to 1377.

30 In suffering thus thy brother to be slaughter'd,
    Thou showest the naked pathway to thy life,
    Teaching stern murder how to butcher thee.
    That which in mean men we entitle patience
    Is pale cold cowardice in noble breasts.
35 What shall I say? To safeguard thine own life,
    The best way is to venge my Gloucester's death.

JOHN OF GAUNT

    God's is the quarrel; for God's substitute,
    His deputy anointed in His sight,
    Hath caused his death: the which if wrongfully,
40 Let heaven revenge; for I may never lift
    An angry arm against His minister.

DUCHESS

    Where then, alas, may I complain myself?

JOHN OF GAUNT

    To God, the widow's champion and defense.

DUCHESS

    Why, then, I will. Farewell, old Gaunt.
45 Thou goest to Coventry, there to behold
    Our cousin Hereford and fell Mowbray fight.
    O, sit my husband's wrongs on Hereford's spear,
    That it may enter butcher Mowbray's breast!
    Or, if misfortune miss the first career,
50 Be Mowbray's sins so heavy in his bosom,
    They may break his foaming courser's back,
    And throw the rider headlong in the lists,
    A caitiff recreant to my cousin Hereford!
    Farewell, old Gaunt. Thy sometimes brother's wife
55 With her companion grief must end her life.

JOHN OF GAUNT

    Sister, farewell. I must to Coventry.
    As much good stay with thee as go with me!

DUCHESS

    Yet one word more: grief boundeth where it falls,
    Not with the empty hollowness, but weight.

JOHN OF GAUNT

> It's God's quarrel now, because it was his chosen king, who serves as God's deputy on earth, who caused Gloucester's death. If it was a crime, let heaven punish it, because I won't raise a hand against God's minister.

DUCHESS OF GLOUCESTER

> Whom should I complain to then?

JOHN OF GAUNT

> To God, who defends widows.

DUCHESS OF GLOUCESTER

> Why then, I will. Good-bye, old Gaunt. You are going to Coventry to see our kinsman Hereford and ruthless Mowbray fight. I hope that the weight of the crime against my husband will give force to Hereford's spear, letting it pierce the killer Mowbray's breast! Or, if he misses in the first attempt, that Mowbray's sins weigh so heavily on him that his horse's back breaks and throws him to the ground! Good-bye, old Gaunt. My grief is so great that I must end my life.

JOHN OF GAUNT

> Sister, good-bye. I have to go to Coventry. May we both fare well!

DUCHESS OF GLOUCESTER

> Just one more word. When grief falls, it rises again, even though it is heavy and not light and empty. I've said

60 I take my leave before I have begun,
    For sorrow ends not when it seemeth done.
    Commend me to thy brother, Edmund York.
    Lo, this is all. Nay, yet depart not so.
    Though this be all, do not so quickly go.
65 I shall remember more. Bid him—ah, what?—
    With all good speed at Plashy visit me.
    Alack, and what shall good old York there see
    But empty lodgings and unfurnish'd walls,
    Unpeopled offices, untrodden stones?
70 And what hear there for welcome but my groans?
    Therefore commend me; let him not come there,
    To seek out sorrow that dwells everywhere.
    Desolate, desolate, will I hence and die.
    The last leave of thee takes my weeping eye.

                                        Exeunt severally

good-bye before I said everything that I wanted to say.
Give my respects to your brother, Edmund York. That's
all, but wait—don't leave yet! I'll think of something else.
Tell him—what?—tell him to visit me at Plashy soon.
Sadly, what will he see there but empty servants' quarters,
bare walls, and floors that no one walks on? What will he
hear as a welcome but my groans? So give my greetings,
but don't tell him to visit me there, since he can find
sorrow easily enough elsewhere. I'll go and die alone,
and now I weep, having to finally say good-bye to you.

They exit separately.

ACT 1, SCENE 3

The lists at Coventry. Enter the LORD MARSHAL *and the*
DUKE OF AUMERLE

LORD MARSHAL
My Lord Aumerle, is Harry Hereford arm'd?

DUKE OF AUMERLE
Yea, at all points, and longs to enter in.

LORD MARSHAL
The Duke of Norfolk, sprightfully and bold,
Stays but the summons of the appellant's trumpet.

DUKE OF AUMERLE
5   Why, then, the champions are prepared, and stay
For nothing but his majesty's approach.

The trumpets sound, and KING RICHARD *enters with his
nobles,* JOHN OF GAUNT, *Bushy, Bagot, Green, and others.
When they are set, enter* THOMAS MOWBRAY *in arms,
defendant, with a* HERALD

KING RICHARD II
Marshal, demand of yonder champion
The cause of his arrival here in arms:
Ask him his name and orderly proceed
10   To swear him in the justice of his cause.

LORD MARSHAL
In God's name and the king's, say who thou art
And why thou comest thus knightly clad in arms,
Against what man thou comest, and what thy quarrel.
Speak truly, on thy knighthood and thy oath;
15   As so defend thee heaven and thy valor!

THOMAS MOWBRAY
My name is Thomas Mowbray, Duke of Norfolk,
Who hither come engaged by my oath—

ACT 1, SCENE 3

The jousting fields at Coventry. The LORD MARSHAL *and the* DUKE OF AUMERLE *enter.*

LORD MARSHAL

Lord Aumerle, does **Harry Hereford** have his weapons?

> Henry Bolingbroke, the Duke of Hereford, was also known as "Harry."

DUKE OF AUMERLE

Yes, completely, and he wants to begin.

LORD MARSHAL

The spirited and bold Duke of Norfolk is just waiting for his accuser's summons.

DUKE OF AUMERLE

Why, then, they are both ready, and we're only waiting on the king's entrance.

Trumpets blow. KING RICHARD II *enters with* JOHN OF GAUNT, BUSHY, BAGOT, GREEN, *and others. Once they are seated,* THOMAS MOWBRAY *enters with his weapons. A herald also enters.*

KING RICHARD II

Marshal, ask the combatant why he's come here with weapons. Ask him his name and make him swear in accordance with the rules that his mission is one of justice.

LORD MARSHAL

In God's name and the king's, tell us who you are and why you have come here with armor and weapons. Who is your opponent, and what is your quarrel? Tell us the truth, as you've sworn on your knighthood. Make your defense.

THOMAS MOWBRAY

My name is Thomas Mowbray, the Duke of Norfolk. I've come as I had sworn to— God forbid a knight breaks his

Which God defend a knight should violate!—
Both to defend my loyalty and truth
20   To God, my king and my succeeding issue,
Against the Duke of Hereford that appeals me
And, by the grace of God and this mine arm,
To prove him, in defending of myself,
A traitor to my God, my king, and me:
25   And as I truly fight, defend me heaven!

The trumpets sound. Enter HENRY BOLINGBROKE, *appellant,*
in armor, with a HERALD

KING RICHARD II

Marshal, ask yonder knight in arms,
Both who he is and why he cometh hither
Thus plated in habiliments of war,
And formally, according to our law,
30   Depose him in the justice of his cause.

LORD MARSHAL

What is thy name? And wherefore comest thou hither,
Before King Richard in his royal lists?
Against whom comest thou? And what's thy quarrel?
Speak like a true knight, so defend thee heaven!

HENRY BOLINGBROKE

35   Harry of Hereford, Lancaster, and Derby
Am I, who ready here do stand in arms,
To prove, by God's grace and my body's valor,
In lists, on Thomas Mowbray, Duke of Norfolk,
That he is a traitor, foul and dangerous,
40   To God of heaven, King Richard and to me.
And as I truly fight, defend me heaven!

LORD MARSHAL

On pain of death, no person be so bold
Or daring-hardy as to touch the lists,
Except the marshal and such officers
45   Appointed to direct these fair designs.

oath! I'm here both to defend my loyalty and the truth of my testimony to God, my king, and any children that I might have. With the grace of God and my ability to fight, I'll prove that my opponent, the Duke of Hereford, is a traitor to God, the king, and to me. And may heaven protect me, since I fight with honor!

A personal trumpet call is played. **HENRY BOLINGBROKE**, *the accuser, enters, with a herald.*

KING RICHARD II

Marshal, ask that knight who he is and why he is here armed for war. Make him formally testify as to the reason he is here to fight, as our law requires.

LORD MARSHAL

What is your name, and why do you come here in front of King Richard? Who is your opponent? What is your quarrel? Speak like a true knight!

HENRY BOLINGBROKE

I am Harry of Hereford, Lancaster, and Derby. I am ready to prove with my weapons, with God's grace, and with my strength that Thomas Mowbray, Duke of Norfolk, is a foul traitor, dangerous to King Richard and to me. May heaven defend me, since I fight for truth!

LORD MARSHAL

Only the marshal and the appointed officials may direct the proceedings, and any other person foolish enough to enter the field will be put to death.

HENRY BOLINGBROKE

Lord marshal, let me kiss my sovereign's hand,
And bow my knee before his majesty:
For Mowbray and myself are like two men
That vow a long and weary pilgrimage;

50 Then let us take a ceremonious leave
And loving farewell of our several friends.

LORD MARSHAL

The appellant in all duty greets your highness,
And craves to kiss your hand and take his leave.

KING RICHARD II

We will descend and fold him in our arms.

55 Cousin of Hereford, as thy cause is right,
So be thy fortune in this royal fight!
Farewell, my blood, which if today thou shed,
Lament we may, but not revenge thee dead.

HENRY BOLINGBROKE

O, let no noble eye profane a tear

60 For me, if I be gored with Mowbray's spear.
As confident as is the falcon's flight
Against a bird, do I with Mowbray fight.
My loving lord, I take my leave of you;
Of you, my noble cousin, Lord Aumerle;

65 Not sick, although I have to do with death,
But lusty, young, and cheerly drawing breath.
Lo, as at English feasts, so I regreet
The daintiest last, to make the end most sweet.
O thou, the earthly author of my blood,

70 Whose youthful spirit, in me regenerate,
Doth with a twofold vigor lift me up
To reach at victory above my head,
Add proof unto mine armor with thy prayers;
And with thy blessings steel my lance's point,

75 That it may enter Mowbray's waxen coat,
And furbish new the name of John a Gaunt,
Even in the lusty havior of his son.

HENRY BOLINGBROKE

Lord Marshal, let me kiss the king's hand and go on my knee before him. Mowbray and I are about to undertake a challenge similar to a long and difficult journey, so we should say a formal good-bye to our friends.

LORD MARSHAL

The accuser greets your highness and asks to kiss your hand and say good-bye.

KING RICHARD II

I'll step down and embrace him. Cousin of Hereford, insofar as your cause is just, I wish you luck in this fight. Good-bye, my cousin. If you die in this fight, I will grieve, but I won't take revenge.

HENRY BOLINGBROKE

If I am pierced by Mowbray's lance, don't misuse your tears for me. I'm as confident as the hawk is when he hunts the sparrow. My loving king, good-bye, and good-bye my cousin, Lord Aumerle. I'm healthy, young, and alive now, even if I'm close to death. Lastly, I'll say farewell to you, my father, just as at a feast I save the best morsel for the end. Oh my creator, your youthful spirit is reborn in me and energizes me to reach for victory. Give strength to my armor with your prayers, and harden my lance with your blessing, so it will pierce Mowbray's coat of armor. May my brave deeds bring new honor to the name of John of Gaunt.

JOHN OF GAUNT

God in thy good cause make thee prosperous!
Be swift like lightning in the execution,
80   And let thy blows, doubly redoubled,
Fall like amazing thunder on the casque
Of thy adverse pernicious enemy.
Rouse up thy youthful blood; be valiant and live.

HENRY BOLINGBROKE

Mine innocency and Saint George to thrive!

THOMAS MOWBRAY

85   However God or fortune cast my lot,
There lives or dies, true to King Richard's throne,
A loyal, just, and upright gentleman:
Never did captive with a freer heart
Cast off his chains of bondage and embrace
90   His golden uncontroll'd enfranchisement,
More than my dancing soul doth celebrate
This feast of battle with mine adversary.
Most mighty liege, and my companion peers,
Take from my mouth the wish of happy years.
95   As gentle and as jocund as to jest
Go I to fight. Truth hath a quiet breast.

KING RICHARD II

Farewell, my lord. Securely I espy
Virtue with valor couched in thine eye.
Order the trial, marshal, and begin.

LORD MARSHAL

100   Harry of Hereford, Lancaster, and Derby,
Receive thy lance; and God defend the right!

HENRY BOLINGBROKE

Strong as a tower in hope, I cry "Amen."

LORD MARSHAL

Go bear this lance to Thomas, Duke of Norfolk.

FIRST HERALD

Harry of Hereford, Lancaster, and Derby,
105   Stands here for God, his sovereign and himself,

JOHN OF GAUNT

> May God give you success in your good cause! Strike as
> quick as lightning, and let your blows fall like thunder on
> the helmet of your enemy. Be courageous and fierce, and
> stay alive.

HENRY BOLINGBROKE

> My innocence and Saint George will protect me!

THOMAS MOWBRAY

> Whatever God or fate has in store for me, I will live
> or die as a loyal, just, and honest gentleman. I joyfully
> celebrate this battle against my enemy, as much as any
> slave celebrates who takes off his chains and becomes
> free. Most powerful king and my friends, I wish you all
> happiness in the years to come. I go to fight as happily as
> I would join in a celebration, because knowing that I have
> truth on my side makes me feel calm.

KING RICHARD II

> Good-bye, my lord. I see both virtue and courage in you.
> Marshal, let's begin.

LORD MARSHAL

> Henry of Hereford, Lancaster, and Derby, take your
> lance. May God defend the right man!

HENRY BOLINGBROKE

> With strength and hope, I say, amen.

LORD MARSHAL

> Take this lance to Thomas, Duke of Norfolk.

FIRST HERALD

> At the risk of being proved false, here stands Henry of
> Hereford, Lancaster, and Derby to demonstrate that the

On pain to be found false and recreant,
To prove the Duke of Norfolk, Thomas Mowbray,
A traitor to his God, his king and him;
And dares him to set forward to the fight.

SECOND HERALD

110   Here standeth Thomas Mowbray, Duke of Norfolk,
On pain to be found false and recreant,
Both to defend himself and to approve
Henry of Hereford, Lancaster, and Derby,
To God, his sovereign and to him disloyal;
115   Courageously and with a free desire
Attending but the signal to begin.

LORD MARSHAL

Sound, trumpets, and set forward, combatants.

(A charge sounded.)

Stay! The king hath thrown his warder down.

KING RICHARD II

Let them lay by their helmets and their spears,
120   And both return back to their chairs again.
Withdraw with us, and let the trumpets sound
While we return these dukes what we decree.

(A long flourish.)

Draw near,
And list what with our council we have done.
125   For that our kingdom's earth should not be soil'd
With that dear blood which it hath fostered;
And for our eyes do hate the dire aspect
Of civil wounds plowed up with neighbors' sword;
And for we think the eagle-winged pride
130   Of sky-aspiring and ambitious thoughts,
With rival-hating envy, set on you
To wake our peace, which in our country's cradle
Draws the sweet infant breath of gentle sleep;
Which so roused up with boisterous untuned drums,
135   With harsh resounding trumpets' dreadful bray,
And grating shock of wrathful iron arms,

Duke of Norfolk, Thomas Mowbray, is a traitor to his
God, his king, and to him. He dares him to step forward
and fight.

SECOND HERALD

At the risk of being proved false, here stands Thomas
Mowbray, Duke of Norfolk, to defend himself and to
prove that Henry of Hereford is disloyal to God, his king,
and to him. By his own free will and with courage, he
waits for the signal to begin.

LORD MARSHAL

Trumpets, play. Step forward, combatants.

(Trumpets play to signal the charge.)

Stop, the king has thrown down his baton.

KING RICHARD II

Tell them to take off their helmets, lay down their spears,
and come back to their chairs by me. Tell the trumpets to
play until I deliver my decree to these men.

(the trumpets play)

Draw near, and listen to what I have devised with my
council. Our kingdom, where you both grew up, should
not be soiled with your blood, and I hate the spectacle
of settling such quarrels with swords. I think that pride,
ambition, and envy have caused you to disturb the sweet
peace of this country. Once that peace is broken by war
drums and the clash of weapons, relatives will be killing
each other. Therefore, I'm sending you out into distant
territories. You, my cousin Hereford, at the threat of
execution if you return, are banished for ten years.

Might from our quiet confines fright fair peace
And make us wade even in our kindred's blood;
Therefore, we banish you our territories.
140   You, cousin Hereford, upon pain of life,
Till twice five summers have enrich'd our fields
Shall not regreet our fair dominions,
But tread the stranger paths of banishment.

HENRY BOLINGBROKE

Your will be done. This must my comfort be:
145   Sun that warms you here shall shine on me,
And those his golden beams to you here lent
Shall point on me and gild my banishment.

KING RICHARD II

Norfolk, for thee remains a heavier doom,
Which I with some unwillingness pronounce:
150   The sly slow hours shall not determinate
The dateless limit of thy dear exile;
The hopeless word of "never to return"
Breathe I against thee, upon pain of life.

THOMAS MOWBRAY

A heavy sentence, my most sovereign liege,
155   And all unlook'd for from your highness' mouth.
A dearer merit, not so deep a maim
As to be cast forth in the common air,
Have I deserved at your highness' hands.
The language I have learn'd these forty years,
160   My native English, now I must forgo:
And now my tongue's use is to me no more
Than an unstringed viol or a harp,
Or like a cunning instrument cased up,
Or, being open, put into his hands
165   That knows no touch to tune the harmony.
Within my mouth you have enjailed my tongue,
Doubly portcullis'd with my teeth and lips;
And dull unfeeling barren ignorance
Is made my jailer to attend on me.

HENRY BOLINGBROKE

> I will do as you command. My comfort in my banishment will be the thought that the same sun that shines on you will shine on me wherever I am.

KING RICHARD II

> Norfolk, I reluctantly must give you a harsher sentence. Your absence won't be marked by a certain number of hours. I must banish you for life.

THOMAS MOWBRAY

> It's a heavy sentence, my lord, and I didn't expect to hear you say that. I deserved to be rewarded, not punished so harshly with exile. I'll have to abandon my native English language, which I've spoken for forty years. My tongue will be of as little use as a broken violin. You've imprisoned it, and ignorance will be my jailer. I'm too old to learn anything new. You've sentenced me to die in silence.

170 I am too old to fawn upon a nurse,
 Too far in years to be a pupil now.
 What is thy sentence then but speechless death,
 Which robs my tongue from breathing native breath?

KING RICHARD II

 It boots thee not to be compassionate:
175 After our sentence plaining comes too late.

THOMAS MOWBRAY

 Then thus I turn me from my country's light,
 To dwell in solemn shades of endless night.

KING RICHARD II

 Return again, and take an oath with thee.
 Lay on our royal sword your banish'd hands.
180 Swear by the duty that you owe to God—
 Our part therein we banish with yourselves—
 To keep the oath that we administer:
 You never shall, so help you truth and God!
 Embrace each other's love in banishment;
185 Nor never look upon each other's face;
 Nor never write, regreet, nor reconcile
 This louring tempest of your home-bred hate;
 Nor never by advised purpose meet
 To plot, contrive, or complot any ill
190 'Gainst us, our state, our subjects, or our land.

HENRY BOLINGBROKE

 I swear.

THOMAS MOWBRAY

 And I, to keep all this.

HENRY BOLINGBROKE

 Norfolk, so far as to mine enemy:
 By this time, had the king permitted us,
195 One of our souls had wander'd in the air.
 Banish'd this frail sepulcher of our flesh,
 As now our flesh is banish'd from this land.
 Confess thy treasons ere thou fly the realm.
 Since thou hast far to go, bear not along
200 The clogging burthen of a guilty soul.

KING RICHARD II

It doesn't help to despair, and once my sentence is
handed out it is too late to lament.

THOMAS MOWBRAY

Then I'll turn away from the light of this country and
resign myself to darkness.

KING RICHARD II

Come back, and take an oath. Put your hands on my
sword and swear this by your duty to God—since your
duty to me will end with your banishment—that you will
never greet each other in exile, or write to each other, or
make up with each other, and that you won't plot any
foul deed against me, my country, my subjects, or any of
my land.

HENRY BOLINGBROKE

I swear.

THOMAS MOWBRAY

So do I.

HENRY OF BOLINGBROKE

If the king had allowed us to fight, Norfolk my enemy,
one of us would be dead by now. One of our souls would
have been banished from its body, just as our bodies are
now banished from this country. Confess your treason
before you go. Don't take the cumbersome burden of
those sins with you.

THOMAS MOWBRAY

No, Bolingbroke: if ever I were traitor,
My name be blotted from the book of life,
And I from heaven banish'd as from hence!
But what thou art, God, thou, and I do know,
205   And all too soon, I fear, the king shall rue.
Farewell, my liege. Now no way can I stray;
Save back to England, all the world's my way.

Exit

KING RICHARD II

Uncle, even in the glasses of thine eyes
I see thy grieved heart. Thy sad aspect
210   Hath from the number of his banish'd years
Pluck'd four away.
(*to* **HENRY BOLINGBROKE**) Six frozen winter spent,
Return with welcome home from banishment.

HENRY BOLINGBROKE

How long a time lies in one little word!
215   Four lagging winters and four wanton springs
End in a word: such is the breath of kings.

JOHN OF GAUNT

I thank my liege that in regard of me
He shortens four years of my son's exile.
But little vantage shall I reap thereby;
220   For, ere the six years that he hath to spend
Can change their moons and bring their times about
My oil-dried lamp and time-bewasted light
Shall be extinct with age and endless night;
My inch of taper will be burnt and done,
225   And blindfold death not let me see my son.

KING RICHARD II

Why uncle, thou hast many years to live.

JOHN OF GAUNT

But not a minute, king, that thou canst give.
Shorten my days thou canst with sullen sorrow,

THOMAS MOWBRAY

No, Bolingbroke. If I were ever a traitor, may I die and be forbidden from heaven! But you and I and God all know what you are, and I fear that the king will find out all too soon—to his sorrow. Good-bye, my lord. Now I'm unable to lose my way, since my way is anywhere in the world other than England.

He exits.

KING RICHARD II

Uncle, I can see in your eyes how much you are grieving. Since you are so sad, I'll reduce your son's exile by four years.
(*to Henry Bolingbroke*) After six years, you will be welcome to come home.

HENRY BOLINGBROKE

How much time is kept in a word! Four slow winters and four lush springs taken away in a word. That's the power of a king.

JOHN OF GAUNT

Thank you, my lord, for shortening my son's exile for my sake. But I won't gain much by it. By the time six years have passed I will be dead and won't be able to see my son.

KING RICHARD II

Why, uncle, you have many years left to live.

JOHN OF GAUNT

But you can't give me an extra minute of life. You can shorten my days by adding this sorrow, but you can't

And pluck nights from me, but not lend a morrow.
230 Thou canst help time to furrow me with age,
But stop no wrinkle in his pilgrimage.
Thy word is current with him for my death,
But dead, thy kingdom cannot buy my breath.

KING RICHARD II

Thy son is banish'd upon good advice,
235 Whereto thy tongue a party verdict gave.
Why at our justice seem'st thou then to lour?

JOHN OF GAUNT

Things sweet to taste prove in digestion sour.
You urged me as a judge, but I had rather
You would have bid me argue like a father.
240 O, had it been a stranger, not my child,
To smooth his fault I should have been more mild.
A partial slander sought I to avoid,
And in the sentence my own life destroy'd.
Alas, I look'd when some of you should say,
245 I was too strict to make mine own away.
But you gave leave to my unwilling tongue
Against my will to do myself this wrong.

KING RICHARD II

Cousin, farewell; and, uncle, bid him so.
Six years we banish him, and he shall go.

Flourish. Exeunt KING RICHARD II *and train*

DUKE OF AUMERLE

250 Cousin, farewell. What presence must not know,
From where you do remain let paper show.

LORD MARSHAL

My lord, no leave take I; for I will ride,
As far as land will let me, by your side.

JOHN OF GAUNT

O, to what purpose dost thou hoard thy words,
255 That thou return'st no greeting to thy friends?

add any time. You can cause me to furrow my brow, but
you can't stop a wrinkle from forming. You can order my
death with a word, but once I'm dead, nothing can be
done to give me another breath.

KING RICHARD II
Banishing your son was a good solution, and you agreed
to it. Why now do you look so gloomy at my justice?

JOHN OF GAUNT
Sometimes a thing that tastes sweet later makes you feel
sick. You asked me to be a judge, but I would rather have
argued as a father. If it had been a stranger rather than
my son, I would have been milder. I wanted to avoid
seeming soft, and, in the process, destroyed myself. Alas,
I expected someone to say I was too strict in banishing
my own son, but you let me agree to this terrible decision.

KING RICHARD II
Cousin, farewell. Uncle, say good-bye, too. I've banished
him for six years, and he must go.

Trumpets blow. KING RICHARD II *and his assistants exit.*

DUKE OF AUMERLE
Cousin, good-bye. Send me a letter telling me where you
are, since I won't be able to hear it from you in person.

LORD MARSHAL
My lord, I won't say good-bye. I'll ride with you as far as
I can.

JOHN OF GAUNT
Why are you remaining silent? Won't you say good-bye
to your friends?

HENRY BOLINGBROKE
>   I have too few to take my leave of you,
>   When the tongue's office should be prodigal
>   To breathe the abundant dolor of the heart.

JOHN OF GAUNT
>   Thy grief is but thy absence for a time.

HENRY BOLINGBROKE
260   Joy absent, grief is present for that time.

JOHN OF GAUNT
>   What is six winters? They are quickly gone.

HENRY BOLINGBROKE
>   To men in joy, but grief makes one hour ten.

JOHN OF GAUNT
>   Call it a travel that thou takest for pleasure.

HENRY BOLINGBROKE
>   My heart will sigh when I miscall it so,
265   Which finds it an enforced pilgrimage.

JOHN OF GAUNT
>   The sullen passage of thy weary steps
>   Esteem as foil wherein thou art to set
>   The precious jewel of thy home return.

HENRY BOLINGBROKE
>   Nay, rather, every tedious stride I make
270   Will but remember me what a deal of world
>   I wander from the jewels that I love.
>   Must I not serve a long apprenticehood
>   To foreign passages, and in the end,
>   Having my freedom, boast of nothing else
275   But that I was a journeyman to grief?

JOHN OF GAUNT
>   All places that the eye of heaven visits
>   Are to a wise man ports and happy havens.
>   Teach thy necessity to reason thus;
>   There is no virtue like necessity.
280   Think not the king did banish thee,

HENRY BOLING BROKE

I should be able to tell you in several ways how sad I feel, but I have no words to express how sad I feel in saying good-bye to you.

JOHN OF GAUNT

Your grief is just that you'll be absent for a time.

HENRY BOLINGBROKE

With joy gone, grief will take up that whole time.

JOHN OF GAUNT

Six years will go by quickly.

HENRY BOLINGBROKE

To a happy man they would pass quickly, but with sorrow one hour feels like ten.

JOHN OF GAUNT

Think of it as a pleasure trip.

HENRY BOLINGBROKE

To pretend it is a vacation will only make it worse.

JOHN OF GAUNT

Think of these sorrowful years as a way to make your return home even happier.

HENRY BOLINGBROKE

No, every step I take away will only remind me how far I am from what I love. I'll be serving so many long years in a foreign land, and, other than my freedom, I'll have nothing to show for it at the end.

JOHN OF GAUNT

A wise man knows that anywhere heaven looks down upon is a refuge. Force yourself to think this way, because you have to. Don't think that the king banished you, but rather that you are the king. Sorrow weighs heaviest on those who bear it timidly. Pretend I sent you to go prove

But thou the king. Woe doth the heavier sit,
Where it perceives it is but faintly borne.
Go, say I sent thee forth to purchase honor
And not the king exiled thee. Or suppose
285 Devouring pestilence hangs in our air
And thou art flying to a fresher clime.
Look what thy soul holds dear, imagine it
To lie that way thou go'st, not whence thou comest.
Suppose the singing birds musicians,
290 The grass whereon thou tread'st the presence strew'd,
The flowers fair ladies, and thy steps no more
Than a delightful measure or a dance;
For gnarling sorrow hath less power to bite
The man that mocks at it and sets it light.

HENRY BOLINGBROKE

295 O, who can hold a fire in his hand
By thinking on the frosty Caucasus?
Or cloy the hungry edge of appetite
By bare imagination of a feast?
Or wallow naked in December snow
300 By thinking on fantastic summer's heat?
O, no! The apprehension of the good
Gives but the greater feeling to the worse.
Fell sorrow's tooth doth never rankle more
Than when he bites, but lanceth not the sore.

JOHN OF GAUNT

305 Come, come, my son, I'll bring thee on thy way.
Had I thy youth and cause, I would not stay.

HENRY BOLINGBROKE

Then, England's ground, farewell; sweet soil, adieu;
My mother, and my nurse, that bears me yet!
Where'er I wander, boast of this I can,
310 Though banish'd, yet a trueborn Englishman.

Exeunt

yourself, not that the king banished you. Or pretend that there is a plague here and that you are seeking a healthier place. Imagine that what you want the most can be found in the direction you are going, not the direction you're coming from. Pretend the birds are musicians, the flowers along your path are fair ladies, and your steps are a dance. Sorrow has no power to hurt the man who makes fun of it and who keeps a sense of humor.

HENRY OF BOLINGBROKE

Who can hold a flame by pretending that it is ice? Or satisfy hunger just by thinking about a feast? Or roll in the snow naked by imagining the heat of summer? Oh, no! Imagining the best only makes the worst harder to bear. Sorrow hurts most when you treat the pain it creates without curing the cause.

JOHN OF GAUNT

Come, come, my son, I'll put you on your way. If I were young enough, I wouldn't remain here.

HENRY OF BOLINGBROKE

Then good-bye, England's earth. Good-bye, sweet soil, my motherland. Wherever I go, I can boast that I am a true Englishman, even if I am banished.

They exit.

ACT 1, SCENE 4

The court. Enter KING RICHARD II, *with* BAGOT *and* GREEN *at one door; and the* DUKE OF AUMERLE *at another*

KING RICHARD II

We did observe. Cousin Aumerle,
How far brought you high Hereford on his way?

DUKE OF AUMERLE

I brought high Hereford, if you call him so,
But to the next highway, and there I left him.

KING RICHARD II

5   And say, what store of parting tears were shed?

DUKE OF AUMERLE

Faith, none for me, except the northeast wind,
Which then blew bitterly against our faces,
Awaked the sleeping rheum, and so by chance
Did grace our hollow parting with a tear.

KING RICHARD II

10   What said our cousin when you parted with him?

DUKE OF AUMERLE

"Farewell."
And, for my heart disdained that my tongue
Should so profane the word, that taught me craft
To counterfeit oppression of such grief
15   That words seem'd buried in my sorrow's grave.
Marry, would the word "farewell" have lengthen'd hours
And added years to his short banishment,
He should have had a volume of farewells;
But since it would not, he had none of me.

KING RICHARD II

20   He is our cousin, cousin, but 'tis doubt,
When time shall call him home from banishment,
Whether our kinsman come to see his friends.
Ourself and Bushy, Bagot here and Green

ACT 1, SCENE 4

King Richard II's palace. KING RICHARD II *enters.* BAGOT *and*
GREEN *stand at one door, and the* DUKE OF AUMERLE *stands
at another.*

KING RICHARD II

How far did you escort proud Hereford?

DUKE OF AUMERLE

I took proud Hereford, if you want to call him that, just
to the next highway and left him there.

KING RICHARD II

And how many tears were shed?

DUKE OF AUMERLE

Honestly, none on my part. Although the wind was
blowing bitterly against our faces, making our eyes water.
I suppose by chance that made me shed some tears.

KING RICHARD II

What did my cousin say when you left him?

DUKE OF AUMERLE

"Good-bye." But I didn't say it back, because that word
has always been a way to disguise my grief when leaving
someone, and I certainly didn't have any grief to disguise
this time. In fact, if saying good-bye would have made
hours longer and added years to his banishment, I would
have given him many good-byes. But I knew that it
wouldn't, so I gave him none.

KING RICHARD II

He is our cousin, cousin. But I doubt that he'll come
see his relatives when he returns home from his exile.
Bushy, Bagot, Green, and I watched how he courts the
common people, and he seems to endear himself to them

          Observed his courtship to the common people;

25   How he did seem to dive into their hearts

          With humble and familiar courtesy,

          What reverence he did throw away on slaves,

          Wooing poor craftsmen with the craft of smiles

          And patient underbearing of his fortune,

30   As 'twere to banish their affects with him.

          Off goes his bonnet to an oyster-wench;

          A brace of draymen bid God speed him well

          And had the tribute of his supple knee,

          With "Thanks, my countrymen, my loving friends,"

35   As were our England in reversion his,

          And he our subjects' next degree in hope.

GREEN

          Well, he is gone; and with him go these thoughts.

          Now for the rebels which stand out in Ireland,

          Expedient manage must be made, my liege,

40   Ere further leisure yield them further means

          For their advantage and your highness' loss.

KING RICHARD II

          We will ourself in person to this war:

          And, for our coffers, with too great a court

          And liberal largess, are grown somewhat light,

45   We are inforced to farm our royal realm;

          The revenue whereof shall furnish us

          For our affairs in hand: if that come short,

          Our substitutes at home shall have blank charters;

          Whereto, when they shall know what men are rich,

50   They shall subscribe them for large sums of gold

          And send them after to supply our wants;

          For we will make for Ireland presently.

          Enter BUSHY

          Bushy, what news?

with humble courtesy. He wasted reverence on slaves
and courted poor craftsman with smiles and a patient
acceptance of his fate, as though he were hoping to take
their affection with him into exile. He took off his hat
to a woman selling oysters. Several oxen drivers blessed
his journey, and he went on one knee and told them,
"Thanks, my countrymen, my loving friends." It was
as though my England were his and my subjects were
placing their hope in him.

GREEN

Well, he is gone, and any thoughts like that go with him.
Now we must make an urgent plan to deal with the rebels
in Ireland, my lord, before giving them time to act gives
them an advantage and puts you at a loss.

KING RICHARD II

I'll go in person to this war. The size of my court and
my generosity have depleted the treasury, so we need to
lease out our right to tax the people. The revenue from
that will keep the country running. If that doesn't bring
in enough, then my deputies here will have authority to
make the rich lords turn over however much of their gold
we choose to supply what we need. I'll leave for Ireland
at once.

BUSHY enters.

Bushy, what is the news?

BUSHY

Old John of Gaunt is grievous sick, my lord,
55   Suddenly taken, and hath sent post haste
To entreat your majesty to visit him.

KING RICHARD II

Where lies he?

BUSHY

At Ely House.

KING RICHARD II

Now put it, God, in the physician's mind
60   To help him to his grave immediately!
The lining of his coffers shall make coats
To deck our soldiers for these Irish wars.
Come, gentlemen, let's all go visit him.
Pray God we may make haste and come too late!

ALL

65   Amen.

Exeunt

BUSHY

> Old John of Gaunt is suddenly very ill, my lord. He
> sent word asking that your majesty visit him as soon as
> possible.

KING RICHARD II

> Where is he?

BUSHY

> At Ely House.

KING RICHARD II

> God, let the physician help him die quickly! His fortune
> will pay for the soldiers' coats in this Irish war. Come,
> gentleman, let's go visit him. Let's hurry, but pray we still
> arrive too late!

ALL

> Amen.

They exit.

ACT TWO
SCENE 1

Ely House. Enter JOHN OF GAUNT *sick, with the* DUKE OF YORK, *& c*

JOHN OF GAUNT

Will the king come, that I may breathe my last
In wholesome counsel to his unstaid youth?

DUKE OF YORK

Vex not yourself, nor strive not with your breath;
For all in vain comes counsel to his ear.

JOHN OF GAUNT

5   O, but they say the tongues of dying men
Enforce attention like deep harmony.
Where words are scarce, they are seldom spent in vain,
For they breathe truth that breathe their words in pain.
He that no more must say is listen'd more
10   Than they whom youth and ease have taught to glose.
More are men's ends mark'd than their lives before:
The setting sun, and music at the close,
As the last taste of sweets, is sweetest last,
Writ in remembrance more than things long past.
15   Though Richard my life's counsel would not hear,
My death's sad tale may yet undeaf his ear.

DUKE OF YORK

No, it is stopp'd with other flattering sounds,
As praises, of whose taste the wise are feared,
Lascivious meters, to whose venom sound
20   The open ear of youth doth always listen;
Report of fashions in proud Italy,
Whose manners still our tardy apish nation
Limps after in base imitation.
Where doth the world thrust forth a vanity—
25   So it be new, there's no respect how vile—

ACT TWO
SCENE 1

Ely Palace, London. **JOHN OF GAUNT**, *who is very sick, and the* **DUKE OF YORK**, *as well as a few assistants, enter.*

JOHN OF GAUNT

Is the young, wild king going to come visit me so I can give him my last words of advice before I die?

DUKE OF YORK

Don't waste the little strength you have worrying about that. Even if he did come, the king doesn't listen to advice.

JOHN OF GAUNT

But people say the words spoken by dying men are usually listened to very closely. When a dying man can hardly talk, he won't speak just for the fun of it. If he talks, he must have something important to say. The young are often ignored because their advice isn't sound. Also, in general, people pay more attention at the end of somebody's life. It's just like the last bite of dessert—it's the sweetest part, the part you try to make last, and the part you remember most. So, even though King Richard ignored me throughout my life, maybe he'll listen to me now that I am dying.

DUKE OF YORK

No, he won't listen—his ears are stuffed with all the sounds that make him happy, like the flattery and praise he receives, which wise men know to be wary of. He also likes raunchy poems, which immature young people always listen to. And he listens to the fashion reports from Italy, which England is always copying and always shamefully trying to catch up to. As long as it is new, no matter how awful it is, it instantly grabs Richard's attention. His desire for all of these things doesn't allow

That is not quickly buzzed into his ears?
Then all too late comes counsel to be heard,
Where will doth mutiny with wit's regard.
Direct not him whose way himself will choose.
30   'Tis breath thou lack'st, and that breath wilt thou lose.

JOHN OF GAUNT

Methinks I am a prophet new inspired
And thus expiring do foretell of him:
His rash fierce blaze of riot cannot last,
For violent fires soon burn out themselves;
35   Small showers last long, but sudden storms are short;
He tires betimes that spurs too fast betimes;
With eager feeding food doth choke the feeder:
Light vanity, insatiate cormorant,
Consuming means, soon preys upon itself.
40   This royal throne of kings, this scepter'd isle,
This earth of majesty, this seat of Mars,
This other Eden, demi-paradise,
This fortress built by Nature for herself
Against infection and the hand of war,
45   This happy breed of men, this little world,
This precious stone set in the silver sea,
Which serves it in the office of a wall,
Or as a moat defensive to a house,
Against the envy of less happier lands,
50   This blessed plot, this earth, this realm, this England,
This nurse, this teeming womb of royal kings,
Fear'd by their breed and famous by their birth,
Renowned for their deeds as far from home,
For Christian service and true chivalry,
55   As is the sepulcher in stubborn Jewry,
Of the world's ransom, blessed Mary's Son,
This land of such dear souls, this dear dear land,
Dear for her reputation through the world,
Is now leased out—I die pronouncing it—
60   Like to a tenement or pelting farm.

him to listen to good advice. Don't give him direction, because he chooses his own course. You'll just be wasting your precious breath.

JOHN OF GAUNT

As I lie here dying, I think that God is suddenly letting me see the king's future. The king can't go on living a wasteful lifestyle forever, in the same way that a raging fire will eventually burn itself out. Little rainstorms often go on for a long time, but big, violent thunderstorms come and go quickly. The person who starts off too fast will soon tire out, and the person who eats too fast will choke on his food. The hungry bird that can't get enough to eat will soon eat itself. This kingdom, this majestic Earth, this paradise, this fortress that Nature built to protect herself against disease and war, this lucky race of people, this little world, this precious jewel of an island sitting in the sea—which protects it like a wall or a moat against the evil intentions of less fortunate countries—this blessed land, this England, this fertile mother of kings who are feared and famous for their Christian actions throughout the world, this land of such good people, this wonderful, wonderful land—it is now rented out, and I'm going to have to die watching it happen. England is surrounded by an ocean whose rocky shore has always pushed back the raging waters. Now, though, England is bound in shame by legal papers, made of rotting parchment and covered in inky blots, that were signed to rent it out. England, which is used to conquering other countries, has now shamefully conquered itself. Oh, how I wish this scandal would die and go away, just like I'm about to die. How happy my death would be then!

England, bound in with the triumphant sea
Whose rocky shore beats back the envious siege
Of watery Neptune, is now bound in with shame,
With inky blots and rotten parchment bonds.
65   That England, that was wont to conquer others,
Hath made a shameful conquest of itself.
Ah, would the scandal vanish with my life,
How happy then were my ensuing death!

Enter KING RICHARD II *and* QUEEN, DUKE OF AUMERLE,
BUSHY, GREEN, BAGOT, LORD ROSS, *and* LORD WILLOUGHBY

DUKE OF YORK
The king is come. Deal mildly with his youth,
70   For young hot colts being raged do rage the more.

QUEEN
How fares our noble uncle Lancaster?
KING RICHARD II
What comfort, man? How is't with aged Gaunt?
JOHN OF GAUNT
O how that name befits my composition!
Old Gaunt indeed, and gaunt in being old.
75   Within me grief hath kept a tedious fast,
And who abstains from meat that is not gaunt?
For sleeping England long time have I watch'd;
Watching breeds leanness, leanness is all gaunt.
The pleasure that some fathers feed upon,
80   Is my strict fast—I mean, my children's looks—
And therein fasting, hast thou made me gaunt.
Gaunt am I for the grave, gaunt as a grave,
Whose hollow womb inherits nought but bones.
KING RICHARD II
Can sick men play so nicely with their names?

KING RICHARD II, *the* QUEEN, *the* DUKE OF AUMERLE, BUSHY, GREEN, BAGOT, LORD ROSS, *and* LORD WILLOUGHBY *enter.*

DUKE OF YORK

(*to John of Gaunt*) The king is here. Go easy with him. He is young and easy to make angry, and if you give him a hard time, you're likely to do nothing but make him angrier.

QUEEN

How are you, John of Gaunt?

KING RICHARD II

Yes, John of Gaunt, tell us how you are.

JOHN OF GAUNT

Oh, how my name fits my condition, and I feel gaunt. I am gaunt because of my old age. And who can go without food and not be gaunt? I have stayed awake and watched England crumble for a long time, and from all the lack of sleep I've grown gaunt. Fathers receive nourishment from seeing their children, and since I can't see my child it has made me gaunt. I'm ready for my grave, and when I'm laid in it, I'll be nothing but bones.

KING RICHARD II

Can men who are really sick play so subtly with their names?

JOHN OF GAUNT

85   No, misery makes sport to mock itself.
      Since thou dost seek to kill my name in me,
      I mock my name, great king, to flatter thee.

KING RICHARD II

      Should dying men flatter with those that live?

JOHN OF GAUNT

      No, no, men living flatter those that die.

KING RICHARD II

90   Thou, now a-dying, say'st thou flatterest me.

JOHN OF GAUNT

      O, no! Thou diest, though I the sicker be.

KING RICHARD II

      I am in health, I breathe, and see thee ill.

JOHN OF GAUNT

      Now He that made me knows I see thee ill;
      Ill in myself to see, and in thee seeing ill.
95   Thy deathbed is no lesser than thy land
      Wherein thou liest in reputation sick;
      And thou, too careless patient as thou art,
      Commit'st thy anointed body to the cure
      Of those physicians that first wounded thee.
100   A thousand flatterers sit within thy crown,
      Whose compass is no bigger than thy head;
      And yet, encaged in so small a verge,
      The waste is no whit lesser than thy land.
      O, had thy grandsire with a prophet's eye
105   Seen how his son's son should destroy his sons,
      From forth thy reach he would have laid thy shame,
      Deposing thee before thou wert possess'd,
      Which art possess'd now to depose thyself.
      Why, cousin, wert thou regent of the world,
110   It were a shame to let this land by lease;
      But for thy world enjoying but this land,
      Is it not more than shame to shame it so?

JOHN OF GAUNT

> Misery likes to make fun of itself. And I thought you might enjoy listening to me make fun of my name since you are banishing my son, who, of course, shares my name.

KING RICHARD II

> Should dying men try to amuse the living?

JOHN OF GAUNT

> No, no, the living should try to amuse the dying.

KING RICHARD II

> You, who are dying, tell me that you're trying to please me.

JOHN OF GAUNT

> Oh no! You're the one dying, even though I'm sicker.

KING RICHARD II

> I'm in good health. I'm breathing fine, and I can see that you are the one who is sick.

JOHN OF GAUNT

> God knows that I can see the sickness in you. You don't realize it, but your deathbed is actually the country that you've been destroying. And you're too clueless to realize that the people you think will cure you are actually the ones making you sick—those flatterers and yes-men you surround yourself with. You don't even see that your subjects are turning on you. You have laid waste to all of England. If your grandfather had been able to see how you were going to destroy this country, he would have reached into the future and stopped you. My nephew, it is an utter shame to lease parts of England out to others. You aren't the king of England anymore. You are simply the landlord of England, and you—

Landlord of England art thou now, not king.
Thy state of law is bond slave to the law.
115 And thou—

KING RICHARD II

                A lunatic lean-witted fool,
Presuming on an ague's privilege,
Darest with thy frozen admonition
Make pale our cheek, chasing the royal blood
120 With fury from his native residence.
Now, by my seat's right royal majesty,
Wert thou not brother to great Edward's son,
This tongue that runs so roundly in thy head
Should run thy head from thy unreverent shoulders.

JOHN OF GAUNT

125 O, spare me not, my brother Edward's son,
For that I was his father Edward's son;
That blood already, like the pelican,
Hast thou tapp'd out and drunkenly caroused.
My brother Gloucester—plain well-meaning soul,
130 Whom fair befal in heaven 'mongst happy souls!—
May be a precedent and witness good
That thou respect'st not spilling Edward's blood.
Join with the present sickness that I have;
And thy unkindness be like crooked age,
135 To crop at once a too long wither'd flower.
Live in thy shame, but die not shame with thee!
These words hereafter thy tormentors be!
Convey me to my bed, then to my grave.
Love they to live that love and honor have.

Exit, borne off by his Attendants

KING RICHARD II

140 And let them die that age and sullens have,
For both hast thou, and both become the grave.

KING RICHARD II

You idiot, taking advantage of your illness as an opportunity to criticize me. How dare you anger and embarrass me so much that my face has gone pale! If you weren't my uncle—that is, the uncle to the King of England—that wild tongue of yours would result in your head being cut from your disobedient shoulders.

JOHN OF GAUNT

Don't do me any favors because I'm your uncle. You have never before hesitated to spill our family's royal blood. My good and simple brother Gloucester, who had royal blood and is happily in heaven now, is someone you weren't afraid to kill. Like a dead flower, your wicked behavior must be plucked immediately. You have lived a bad life, but you must change your ways before you die. May my words torment you always! (*to his assistants*) Take me to my bed, and then let me die. Let only those who are honorable and loving live happily.

> **JOHN OF GAUNT** *is carried off the stage by his assistants.*

KING RICHARD II

And let those who are old and gloomy die, and you, John of Gaunt, are both.

DUKE OF YORK

I do beseech your majesty, impute his words
To wayward sickliness and age in him:
He loves you, on my life, and holds you dear
145   As Harry, Duke of Hereford, were he here.

KING RICHARD II

Right, you say true: as Hereford's love, so his;
As theirs, so mine; and all be as it is.

Enter **NORTHUMBERLAND**

NORTHUMBERLAND

My liege, old Gaunt commends him to your majesty.

KING RICHARD II

What says he?

NORTHUMBERLAND

150   Nay, nothing; all is said
His tongue is now a stringless instrument;
Words, life and all, old Lancaster hath spent.

DUKE OF YORK

Be York the next that must be bankrupt so!
Though death be poor, it ends a mortal woe.

KING RICHARD II

155   The ripest fruit first falls, and so doth he;
His time is spent, our pilgrimage must be.
So much for that. Now for our Irish wars:
We must supplant those rough rug-headed kerns,
Which live like venom where no venom else
160   But only they have privilege to live.
And for these great affairs do ask some charge,
Towards our assistance we do seize to us
The plate, corn, revenues, and moveables,
Whereof our uncle Gaunt did stand possess'd.

DUKE OF YORK

165   How long shall I be patient? Ah, how long
Shall tender duty make me suffer wrong?

DUKE OF YORK

I beg you, your majesty, blame his words on his age and his sickness. I swear that he loves you and holds you as close to his heart as he does Harry Duke of Hereford.

KING RICHARD II

Right, what you say is true. Just as Harry holds me close to his heart, John of Gaunt must hold me also. And, in turn, I love both of them. That's how it is.

NORTHUMBERLAND *enters.*

NORTHUMBERLAND

My lord, Gaunt sends his regards to you.

KING RICHARD II

What did he say?

NORTHUMBERLAND

Actually, he didn't say anything. He can't talk. He has died.

DUKE OF YORK

I hope that I will be the next to die! Death is terrible, but at least it stops the pain of living.

KING RICHARD II

Gaunt is the first to die, just like the ripest fruit is always the first to fall off the tree. Well, that's over with. Now, about the war in Ireland. We must get rid of those shaggy-haired Irish soldiers who live there. Let's seize all of Gaunt's money and property to help pay for the war.

DUKE OF YORK

How long can I hold out? How long will my obligation to the king make me suffer these wrongs

Not Gloucester's death, nor Hereford's banishment.
Not Gaunt's rebukes, nor England's private wrongs,
Nor the prevention of poor Bolingbroke
170 About his marriage, nor my own disgrace,
Have ever made me sour my patient cheek,
Or bend one wrinkle on my sovereign's face.
I am the last of noble Edward's sons,
Of whom thy father, Prince of Wales, was first.
175 In war was never lion raged more fierce,
In peace was never gentle lamb more mild,
Than was that young and princely gentleman.
His face thou hast, for even so look'd he,
Accomplish'd with the number of thy hours;
180 But when he frown'd, it was against the French
And not against his friends. His noble hand
Did will what he did spend and spent not that
Which his triumphant father's hand had won.
His hands were guilty of no kindred blood,
185 But bloody with the enemies of his kin.
O Richard! York is too far gone with grief,
Or else he never would compare between.

KING RICHARD II
Why, uncle, what's the matter?

DUKE OF YORK
                                    O my liege,
190 Pardon me, if you please. If not, I, pleased
Not to be pardon'd, am content withal.
Seek you to seize and gripe into your hands
The royalties and rights of banish'd Hereford?
Is not Gaunt dead, and doth not Hereford live?
195 Was not Gaunt just, and is not Harry true?
Did not the one deserve to have an heir?
Is not his heir a well-deserving son?
Take Hereford's rights away, and take from time
His charters and his customary rights;
200 Let not tomorrow then ensue today;

against Gaunt? Nothing has ever made me show my
frustrations—not Gloucester's death, nor Hereford's
banishment, nor Gaunt's criticisms, nor the king's
bad treatment of England, nor the **king's refusal to
let Bolingbroke marry**, nor my own ill treatment. I
am the last of Edward's sons. Your father, the Prince
of Wales, was the first. There was never anyone more
fierce in wartime and more gentle in peacetime than
the Prince of Wales. You look just like him when
he was your age. When he got upset, it was against
the French, not against his allies. He spent only
what he'd earned, and he never spent anything that
his father had won. He never did anything wrong
to his countrymen, but he punished his enemies.
Richard, I am too upset, or I would never make these
comparisons.

Richard rejected Bolingbroke's request to marry the King of France's cousin

KING RICHARD II

Why, uncle, what's the matter?

DUKE OF YORK

Oh, my lord, forgive me, please. If you won't, I'll
understand. Do you really want to seize all of Gaunt's
property? He might be dead, but isn't his son still alive?
Wasn't Gaunt a good man, and isn't Harry good, too?
Doesn't Gaunt deserve to have an heir? And isn't Harry
a deserving heir? If you take away Harry's right to inherit
his father's belongings, then you are going against
tradition. It would be like taking away Time's authority
and rights and preventing tomorrow from following
today. Remember, you yourself are a king because you
inherited the position. Now, I swear before God, if you
do this, you will bring all sorts of danger to yourself and

Be not thyself; for how art thou a king
But by fair sequence and succession?
Now, afore God—God forbid I say true!—
If you do wrongfully seize Hereford's rights,
205   Call in the letters patent that he hath
By his attorneys-general to sue
His livery, and deny his offer'd homage,
You pluck a thousand dangers on your head,
You lose a thousand well-disposed hearts
210   And prick my tender patience, to those thoughts
Which honor and allegiance cannot think.

KING RICHARD II

Think what you will, we seize into our hands
His plate, his goods, his money, and his lands.

DUKE OF YORK

I'll not be by the while. My liege, farewell.
215   What will ensue hereof, there's none can tell;
But by bad courses may be understood
That their events can never fall out good.

Exit

KING RICHARD II

Go, Bushy, to the Earl of Wiltshire straight.
Bid him repair to us to Ely House
220   To see this business. Tomorrow next
We will for Ireland; and 'tis time, I trow.
And we create, in absence of ourself,
Our uncle York lord governor of England,
For he is just and always loved us well.
225   Come on, our queen. Tomorrow must we part.
Be merry, for our time of stay is short

Flourish. Exeunt KING RICHARD II, QUEEN, DUKE OF
AUMERLE, BUSHY, GREEN, *and* BAGOT

turn a thousand people against you. You will force me to lose my patience, and I'll think about doing things to you that, because I still honor and obey you, I cannot even think about.

KING RICHARD II

Think whatever you want, but we're going to seize his money and all of his property.

DUKE OF YORK

I won't stand here and watch. Good-bye, my lord. What will happen now, nobody can say. But no good outcome can result from a bad decision like this.

DUKE OF YORK exits.

KING RICHARD II

Bushy, go straight to the Earl of Wiltshire and tell him to come to Ely House to help us. Tomorrow morning we'll go to Ireland. I believe it's time. I'll make my uncle York the Lord Governor of England while I'm away. He is fair and has always loved me very much. Come, my queen, we must leave tomorrow. Be well.

Trumpets blow, as KING RICHARD II, the QUEEN, the DUKE OF AUMERLE, BUSHY, GREEN, and BAGOT exit.

NORTHUMBERLAND

Well, lords, the Duke of Lancaster is dead.

LORD ROSS

And living too, for now his son is duke.

LORD WILLOUGHBY

Barely in title, not in revenue.

NORTHUMBERLAND

230   Richly in both, if justice had her right.

LORD ROSS

My heart is great, but it must break with silence,

Ere't be disburden'd with a liberal tongue.

NORTHUMBERLAND

Nay, speak thy mind, and let him ne'er speak more

That speaks thy words again to do thee harm!

LORD WILLOUGHBY

235   Tends that thou wouldst speak to the Duke of Hereford?

If it be so, out with it boldly, man;

Quick is mine ear to hear of good towards him.

LORD ROSS

No good at all that I can do for him;

Unless you call it good to pity him,

240   Bereft and gelded of his patrimony.

NORTHUMBERLAND

Now, afore God, 'tis shame such wrongs are borne

In him, a royal prince, and many moe

Of noble blood in this declining land.

The king is not himself, but basely led

245   By flatterers; and what they will inform,

Merely in hate, 'gainst any of us all,

That will the king severely prosecute

'Gainst us, our lives, our children, and our heirs.

LORD ROSS

The commons hath he pill'd with grievous taxes,

250   And quite lost their hearts. The nobles hath he fined

For ancient quarrels, and quite lost their hearts.

NORTHUMBERLAND

Well, lords, the Duke of Lancaster is dead.

LORD ROSS

But he also kind of lives because his son is now a duke.

LORD WILLOUGHBY

His son might have the title of duke, but he doesn't have the income of one.

NORTHUMBERLAND

If there were justice in the world, then he would have both the title and the income.

LORD ROSS

I have a lot of troubles on my mind. But I must keep silent about them for now.

NORTHUMBERLAND

Speak your mind. And if anyone uses what you say against you, let that person never speak again!

LORD WILLOUGHBY

Are you going to say something about the Duke of Hereford? If so, say it, man! I am always eager to hear good things about him.

LORD ROSS

I can't do him any good, unless it's good to pity him, since he's now deprived of his inheritance.

NORTHUMBERLAND

With God as my witness, I say it's a shame that such wrongs have been done to him and to others of royal blood in this crumbling land. The king is not acting like himself. He's being deceived by his group of flatterers. Purely out of hatred they make accusations against us, leading the king to persecute us and our children.

LORD ROSS

He's taxed the common people heavily and they've turned against him. He's also fined the nobles for old grudges and turned them against him, as well.

LORD WILLOUGHBY

And daily new exactions are devised,
As blanks, benevolences, and I wot not what.
But what, o' God's name, doth become of this?

NORTHUMBERLAND

255 Wars have not wasted it, for warr'd he hath not,
But basely yielded upon compromise
That which his noble ancestors achieved with blows.
More hath he spent in peace than they in wars.

LORD ROSS

The Earl of Wiltshire hath the realm in farm.

LORD WILLOUGHBY

260 The king's grown bankrupt, like a broken man.

NORTHUMBERLAND

Reproach and dissolution hangeth over him.

LORD ROSS

He hath not money for these Irish wars,
His burthenous taxations notwithstanding,
But by the robbing of the banish'd duke.

NORTHUMBERLAND

265 His noble kinsman. Most degenerate king!
But, lords, we hear this fearful tempest sing,
Yet see no shelter to avoid the storm;
We see the wind sit sore upon our sails,
And yet we strike not, but securely perish.

LORD ROSS

270 We see the very wreck that we must suffer;
And unavoided is the danger now,
For suffering so the causes of our wreck.

NORTHUMBERLAND

Not so. Even through the hollow eyes of death
I spy life peering; but I dare not say
275 How near the tidings of our comfort is.

LORD WILLOUGHBY

Nay, let us share thy thoughts, as thou dost ours.

LORD WILLOUGHBY

> Every day he devises new ways of forcing people to pay, like mandatory loans and I don't know what else. What, in God's name, is he doing with all of this money?

NORTHUMBERLAND

> He hasn't spent the money on wars because he hasn't waged any wars. He has shamefully compromised with our enemies and given away what our ancestors won in battle. He's spent more in peacetime than they did in wartime.

LORD ROSS

> The Earl of Wiltshire has rented out the land.

LORD WILLOUGHBY

> The king is bankrupt.

NORTHUMBERLAND

> He is disgraced.

LORD ROSS

> The only way he can afford to fight the war in Ireland, even with all the money that he's collected from these new taxes, is by stealing everything from the Duke of Hereford.

NORTHUMBERLAND

> Friends, we see this storm coming and yet we don't seek any shelter to avoid it! We see the wind blowing fiercely upon our sails and yet we don't lower the sails but recklessly perish.

LORD ROSS

> We see the shipwreck coming, but the danger is unavoidable now because we sat by and allowed all this to happen.

NORTHUMBERLAND

> That's not true. Even though we are close to ruin, I can see a way out. But I'm not going to say how near the news of our rescue is.

LORD WILLOUGHBY

> Please tell us your thoughts, as we have told you ours.

LORD ROSS

    Be confident to speak, Northumberland:
    We three are but thyself, and, speaking so,
    Thy words are but as thoughts. Therefore, be bold.

NORTHUMBERLAND

280   Then thus: I have from Le Port Blanc, a bay
    In Brittany, received intelligence
    That Harry Duke of Hereford, Rainold Lord Cobham,
    That late broke from the Duke of Exeter,
    His brother, Archbishop late of Canterbury,
285   Sir Thomas Erpingham, Sir John Ramston,
    Sir John Norbery, Sir Robert Waterton, and
        Francis Quoint,
    All these well furnish'd by the Duke of Bretagne
    With eight tall ships, three thousand men of war,
    Are making hither with all due expedience
290   And shortly mean to touch our northern shore:
    Perhaps they had ere this, but that they stay
    The first departing of the king for Ireland.
    If then we shall shake off our slavish yoke,
    Imp out our drooping country's broken wing,
295   Redeem from broking pawn the blemish'd crown,
    Wipe off the dust that hides our scepter's gilt
    And make high majesty look like itself,
    Away with me in post to Ravenspurgh.
    But if you faint, as fearing to do so,
300   Stay and be secret, and myself will go.

LORD ROSS

    To horse, to horse! Urge doubts to them that fear.

LORD WILLOUGHBY

    Hold out my horse, and I will first be there.

Exeunt

LORD ROSS

> Have the confidence to speak, Northumberland. The three of us are just like you. If you speak, you'll most likely say what we're already thinking. Be bold.

NORTHUMBERLAND

> Then here it is: I have learned that the Duke of Bretagne, in Brittany, has given eight large ships to Harry Duke of Hereford as well as Rainold Lord Cobhman—who recently broke his alliance with the Duke of Exeter— his brother, the former Archbishop of Canterbury, Sir Thomas Erpingham, Sir John Ramston, Sir John Norbery, Sir Robert Waterton, and Francis Quoint. These men sailed the ships with three thousand soldiers from Port le Blanc, and right now they are racing to England. They might even have arrived but are waiting for the king to leave for Ireland before landing. If you want to be free of your slavery to the king, help our country to rise again, and restore the honor of our royalty, then come with me right now to Ravenspurgh. If you're afraid to do so, then wait here and be silent while I go myself.

LORD ROSS

> To our horses! Encourage anyone who is scared.

LORD WILLOUGHBY

> If my horse holds up, I'll be the first one there.

They exit.

ACT 2, SCENE 2

The palace. Enter QUEEN, BUSHY, *and* BAGOT

BUSHY

> Madam, your majesty is too much sad.
> You promised, when you parted with the king,
> To lay aside life-harming heaviness
> And entertain a cheerful disposition.

QUEEN

5 > To please the king I did; to please myself
> I cannot do it; yet I know no cause
> Why I should welcome such a guest as grief,
> Save bidding farewell to so sweet a guest
> As my sweet Richard. Yet again, methinks,
10 > Some unborn sorrow, ripe in fortune's womb,
> Is coming towards me, and my inward soul
> With nothing trembles. At some thing it grieves,
> More than with parting from my lord the king.

BUSHY

> Each substance of a grief hath twenty shadows,
15 > Which shows like grief itself, but is not so;
> For sorrow's eye, glazed with blinding tears,
> Divides one thing entire to many objects;
> Like perspectives, which rightly gazed upon
> Show nothing but confusion, eyed awry
20 > Distinguish form: so your sweet majesty,
> Looking awry upon your lord's departure,
> Find shapes of grief, more than himself, to wail;
> Which, look'd on as it is, is nought but shadows
> Of what it is not. Then, thrice-gracious queen,
25 > More than your lord's departure weep not. More's
> not seen;
> Or if it be, 'tis with false sorrow's eye,
> Which for things true weeps things imaginary.

ACT 2, SCENE 2

King Richard II's Palace. The QUEEN, BUSHY, *and* BAGOT *enter.*

BUSHY

> Madam, you are too sad. When we left the king, you
> promised to stop worrying so much and to try to act
> more cheerfully.

QUEEN

> I promised that to make the king happy, but for myself I
> cannot do it. I don't know why I should be so sad, except
> that I had to say good-bye to my sweet Richard. But I
> also think that something bad is going to happen to me
> and I'm inwardly grieving. It's making me more sad than
> the king's leaving does.

BUSHY

> When you're already sad it seems like everything is awful
> and your grief is multiplied. But, in reality, that's not the
> case. Because you're sad, things don't appear to you as
> they actually are, so in your husband's departure you see
> many things to grieve. Those are just shadows. So don't
> cry for anything but your husband's leaving. Any other
> causes of grief are just imaginary.

QUEEN

> It may be so, but yet my inward soul
> Persuades me it is otherwise. Howe'er it be,
> 30   I cannot but be sad; so heavy sad
> As, though on thinking on no thought I think,
> Makes me with heavy nothing faint and shrink.

BUSHY

> 'Tis nothing but conceit, my gracious lady.

QUEEN

> 'Tis nothing less. Conceit is still derived
> 35   From some forefather grief. Mine is not so,
> For nothing had begot my something grief;
> Or something hath the nothing that I grieve.
> 'Tis in reversion that I do possess;
> But what it is, that is not yet known; what
> 40   I cannot name. 'Tis nameless woe, I wot.

Enter GREEN

GREEN

> God save your majesty! And well met, gentlemen.
> I hope the king is not yet shipp'd for Ireland.

QUEEN

> Why hopest thou so? 'Tis better hope he is;
> For his designs crave haste, his haste good hope.
> 45   Then wherefore dost thou hope he is not shipp'd?

GREEN

> That he, our hope, might have retired his power,
> And driven into despair an enemy's hope,
> Who strongly hath set footing in this land.
> The banish'd Bolingbroke repeals himself,
> 50   And with uplifted arms is safe arrived
> At Ravenspurgh.

QUEEN

>   Now God in heaven forbid!

QUEEN

That may be true, but my instinct tells me otherwise. Whatever the case, I feel nothing but grief. In fact, I feel so sad that even when I'm not thinking about anything at all I feel woefully faint and weak.

BUSHY

That's nothing but your imagination, my queen.

QUEEN

Far from it. Imaginary feelings of grief are always the result of some real, prior grief. But that's not my situation, as nothing has happened to me to cause my grief. My grief is reversed: I feel a grief whose cause I haven't experienced yet. But I don't know what that is. I can't name it. All I know is that it's a nameless sadness.

GREEN *enters.*

GREEN

God save the queen! And good to see you, too, gentlemen. I hope the king hasn't left yet for Ireland.

QUEEN

Why do you hope that? It's better if he has, since his plans require that he act quickly. So why do you hope he hasn't sailed?

GREEN

Our hope is that he might have brought his forces back from Ireland and caused our enemy, Bolingbroke, to give up. Even though he is exiled, he has returned to England. He and a strong army have arrived safely to Ravenspurgh ready to fight.

QUEEN

God, no!

GREEN

> Ah, madam, 'tis too true! And that is worse,
> The Lord Northumberland, his son young Henry Percy,
> 55 The Lords of Ross, Beaumond, and Willoughby,
> With all their powerful friends, are fled to him.

BUSHY

> Why have you not proclaim'd Northumberland
> And all the rest revolted faction traitors?

GREEN

> We have: whereupon the Earl of Worcester
> 60 Hath broke his staff, resign'd his stewardship,
> And all the household servants fled with him
> To Bolingbroke.

QUEEN

> So, Green, thou art the midwife to my woe,
> And Bolingbroke my sorrow's dismal heir.
> 65 Now hath my soul brought forth her prodigy,
> And I, a gasping new-deliver'd mother,
> Have woe to woe, sorrow to sorrow join'd.

BUSHY

> Despair not, madam.

QUEEN

>   Who shall hinder me?
> 70 I will despair, and be at enmity
> With cozening hope. He is a flatterer,
> A parasite, a keeper back of death,
> Who gently would dissolve the bands of life,
> Which false hope lingers in extremity.

> *Enter* DUKE OF YORK

GREEN

> 75 Here comes the Duke of York.

GREEN

Madam, it's true, and what's worse is that Lord
Northumberland, his young son Henry Percy, the
Lord of Ross, the Lord of Beaumond, and the Lord of
Willoughby, along with their powerful friends, have all
gone to join him.

BUSHY

Why haven't you proclaimed Northumberland and the
others traitors?

GREEN

We did, and that's when the Earl of Worcester broke
his **staff, resigned his job**, and, along with the
king's servants, fled to join Bolingbroke.

*A staff is a rod of
office and would
have been carried
by the Earl of
Worcester, as the
steward of the
king's household.*

QUEEN

So, Green, you have helped me to give birth: I was
pregnant with sorrow, Bolingbroke is the newborn
child, and I am like a gasping mother who has just
delivered her baby. Now I understand my sense of
sorrow and dread.

BUSHY

Madam, do not despair.

QUEEN

Who's going to stop me? I will despair, and I will not
put up with any false hopes. False hope flatters and feeds
on us, draws out our pain, and withholds death, which
would be gentle otherwise.

The DUKE OF YORK *enters.*

GREEN

Here comes the Duke of York.

QUEEN
> With signs of war about his aged neck.
> O, full of careful business are his looks!
> Uncle, for God's sake, speak comfortable words.

DUKE OF YORK
> Should I do so, I should belie my thoughts.
80 > Comfort's in heaven, and we are on the earth,
> Where nothing lives but crosses, cares, and grief.
> Your husband, he is gone to save far off,
> Whilst others come to make him lose at home.
> Here am I left to underprop his land,
85 > Who, weak with age, cannot support myself.
> Now comes the sick hour that his surfeit made;
> Now shall he try his friends that flatter'd him.

Enter a **SERVANT**

SERVANT
> My lord, your son was gone before I came.

DUKE OF YORK
> He was? Why, so! Go all which way it will!
90 > The nobles they are fled, the commons they are cold,
> And will, I fear, revolt on Hereford's side.
> Sirrah, get thee to Plashy, to my sister Gloucester;
> Bid her send me presently a thousand pound.
> Hold, take my ring.

SERVANT
95 > My lord, I had forgot to tell your lordship,
> Today, as I came by, I called there—
> But I shall grieve you to report the rest.

DUKE OF YORK
> What is't, knave?

SERVANT
> An hour before I came, the duchess died.

QUEEN

His old neck shows signs of war. Oh, his face is full of anxiety! Uncle, for God's sake, give us good news.

DUKE OF YORK

If I were to give you good news, I would be hiding my real thoughts. Good news is in heaven, and we are on earth, where nothing lives but trials, anxieties, and sorrow. Your husband has gone to protect his rule in Ireland, while others have come here to take it from him in England. Here I am, too old to support myself, left to prop up his country. The bad times that we thought his overindulgent ways would bring have arrived. Now his friends will be tested.

A **SERVANT** *enters.*

SERVANT

My lord, your son was gone before I arrived.

DUKE OF YORK

He was? Of course! Things are just happening any way they want! The nobles have fled; the commoners aren't concerned, and they will likely fight on Hereford's side. (*to the servant*) Sir, get thee to Plashy, to my sister-in-law Gloucester. Tell her to send me one thousand pounds right away. Wait, take my **ring**.

SERVANT

My lord, I forgot to tell you, I went by her house today. But it will upset you if I tell you the rest.

To prove the servant comes from the Duke of York.

DUKE OF YORK

What is it, boy?

SERVANT

An hour before I got there, your sister-in-law died.

DUKE OF YORK

100   God for his mercy! What a tide of woes
       Comes rushing on this woeful land at once!
       I know not what to do. I would to God,
       So my untruth had not provoked him to it,
       The king had cut off my head with my brother's.
105   What, are there no posts dispatch'd for Ireland?
       How shall we do for money for these wars?
       Come, sister—cousin, I would say—pray, pardon me.
       Go, fellow, get thee home, provide some carts
       And bring away the armor that is there.

                                          Exit SERVANT

110   Gentlemen, will you go muster men?
       If I know how or which way to order these affairs
       Thus thrust disorderly into my hands,
       Never believe me. Both are my kinsmen:
       The one is my sovereign, whom both my oath
115   And duty bids defend; the other again
       Is my kinsman, whom the king hath wrong'd,
       Whom conscience and my kindred bids to right.
       Well, somewhat we must do. Come, cousin, I'll
       Dispose of you.
120   Gentlemen, go, muster up your men,
       And meet me presently at Berkeley.
       I should to Plashy too;
       But time will not permit. All is uneven,
       And everything is left at six and seven.

                          Exeunt DUKE OF YORK *and* QUEEN

BUSHY

125   The wind sits fair for news to go to Ireland,
       But none returns. For us to levy power
       Proportionable to the enemy
       Is all unpossible.

DUKE OF YORK

God have mercy! What a tide of troubles comes rushing over this land all at once! I don't know what to do. I wish to God that the king had cut off my head when he cut off my brother's. Has no one sent any messengers to Ireland yet? How are we going to pay for these wars? Come, sister—or I should say, cousin. Excuse me. (*to the servant*) Go home, fellow, and find some carts and bring the armor that's there.

The **SERVANT** *exits.*

Gentlemen, will you go round up some men? I don't know what I should do now. Both Richard and Bolingbroke are my kinsmen. One is my king, to whom I've pledged allegiance and have a duty to defend. The other is my kinsman, whom the king has mistreated. My conscience and my family bonds tell me to right those wrongs. Well, we've got to do something. (*to the queen*) Come, cousin, I'll make arrangements for you. Gentlemen, go and round up some men and meet me at Berkeley Castle. I should go to Plashy, too, but there isn't enough time. Everything is in chaos.

The **DUKE OF YORK** *and the* **QUEEN** *exit.*

BUSHY

The message has probably reached Ireland, but no news has come back yet. It's impossible for us to find enough soldiers to match the enemy's force.

GREEN

    Besides, our nearness to the king in love

130   Is near the hate of those love not the king.

BAGOT

    And that's the wavering commons: for their love

    Lies in their purses, and whoso empties them

    By so much fills their hearts with deadly hate.

BUSHY

    Wherein the king stands generally condemn'd.

BAGOT

135   If judgment lie in them, then so do we,

    Because we ever have been near the king.

GREEN

    Well, I will for refuge straight to Bristol Castle.

    The Earl of Wiltshire is already there.

BUSHY

    Thither will I with you; for little office

140   The hateful commons will perform for us,

    Except like curs to tear us all to pieces.

    Will you go along with us?

BAGOT

    No, I will to Ireland to his majesty.

    Farewell. If heart's presages be not vain,

145   We three here art that ne'er shall meet again.

BUSHY

    That's as York thrives to beat back Bolingbroke.

GREEN

    Alas, poor duke! The task he undertakes

    Is numbering sands and drinking oceans dry.

    Where one on his side fights, thousands will fly.

150   Farewell at once, for once, for all, and ever.

BUSHY

    Well, we may meet again.

BAGOT

                   I fear me, never.

Exeunt

GREEN

Besides, our closeness to the king means we are hated by those who hate the king.

BAGOT

And that's how the common folk must be. Their love depends on who gives them money, and they hate those who take their money away.

BUSHY

That's why almost all the common folk hate the king.

BAGOT

If they are to be the judges, then our fate is in their hands, because we've always been on the side of the king.

GREEN

Well, I'm going straight to Bristol Castle to take refuge. The Earl of Wiltshire is already there.

BUSHY

I'll go with you. The hateful common folk won't help us at all but will act like dogs and tear us to pieces. Will you come with us?

BAGOT

No. I'll go to the king in Ireland. Good-bye. If my instinct is correct, the three of us here will never meet again.

BUSHY

That depends on whether York can defeat Bolingbroke.

GREEN

Oh, poor duke! The task he must begin is as hard as counting the sand in a desert or drinking all the water in the ocean. For every person who fights with him, there will be thousands who will not. Good-bye immediately and forever.

BUSHY

Well, we might meet again.

BAGOT

I fear that we won't.

They exit.

ACT 2, SCENE 3

Wilds in Gloucestershire. Enter HENRY BOLINGBROKE *and*
NORTHUMBERLAND, *with Forces*

HENRY BOLINGBROKE
How far is it, my lord, to Berkeley now?

NORTHUMBERLAND
Believe me, noble lord,
I am a stranger here in Gloucestershire.
These high wild hills and rough uneven ways
5   Draws out our miles, and makes them wearisome,
And yet your fair discourse hath been as sugar,
Making the hard way sweet and delectable.
But I bethink me what a weary way
From Ravenspurgh to Cotswold will be found
10   In Ross and Willoughby, wanting your company,
Which, I protest, hath very much beguiled
The tediousness and process of my travel.
But theirs is sweetened with the hope to have
The present benefit which I possess;
15   And hope to joy is little less in joy
Than hope enjoy'd. By this the weary lords
Shall make their way seem short, as mine hath done
By sight of what I have, your noble company.

HENRY BOLINGBROKE
Of much less value is my company
20   Than your good words. But who comes here?

Enter HENRY PERCY

NORTHUMBERLAND
It is my son, young Harry Percy,
Sent from my brother Worcester, whencesoever.
Harry, how fares your uncle?

ACT 2, SCENE 3

In the woods in Gloucestershire. HENRY BOLINGBROKE *and*
NORTHUMBERLAND *enter with an army.*

HENRY BOLINGBROKE

How much farther is it to Berkeley, my lord?

NORTHUMBERLAND

Believe me, my noble lord, I'm a stranger to these parts.
These high and wild hills go on for miles and are tiring.
And yet your good conversation has been like sugar,
making the difficult journey sweeter. But I think it will be
a long and hard journey from Ravenspurgh to Cotswold
for Ross and Willoughby, since they won't have your
company, which has made my trip easier. But their trip
will be made more enjoyable by the expectation that
you'll go with them next time. In this way, the journey
for those tired lords will seem shorter. That's what has
happened to me. My journey has seemed shorter because
you've been with me.

HENRY BOLINGBROKE

My companionship isn't nearly as valuable as your kind
words. Who's coming?

HENRY PERCY *enters.*

NORTHUMBERLAND

It's my son, young Harry Percy. He was sent by my
brother Worcester, wherever he may be. Harry, how is
your uncle Worcester?

HENRY PERCY

> I had thought, my lord, to have learn'd his health of you.

NORTHUMBERLAND

25 Why, is he not with the queen?

HENRY PERCY

> No, my good Lord; he hath forsook the court,
> Broken his staff of office, and dispersed
> The household of the king.

NORTHUMBERLAND

> What was his reason?

30 He was not so resolved when last we spake together.

HENRY PERCY

> Because your lordship was proclaimed traitor.
> But he, my lord, is gone to Ravenspurgh,
> To offer service to the Duke of Hereford,
> And sent me over by Berkeley, to discover

35 What power the Duke of York had levied there;
> Then with directions to repair to Ravenspurgh.

NORTHUMBERLAND

> Have you forgot the Duke of Hereford, boy?

HENRY PERCY

> No, my good lord, for that is not forgot
> Which ne'er I did remember. To my knowledge,

40 I never in my life did look on him.

NORTHUMBERLAND

> Then learn to know him now. This is the duke.

HENRY PERCY

> My gracious lord, I tender you my service,
> Such as it is, being tender, raw and young—
> Which elder days shall ripen and confirm

45 To more approved service and desert.

HENRY BOLINGBROKE

> I thank thee, gentle Percy, and be sure
> I count myself in nothing else so happy
> As in a soul remembering my good friends;
> And, as my fortune ripens with thy love,

HENRY PERCY

> I was thinking, my lord, that you would tell me that.

NORTHUMBERLAND

> Is he not with the queen?

HENRY PERCY

> No, my good lord. He has abandoned the court. He broke his staff and let the king's servants go.

NORTHUMBERLAND

> For what reason? The last time we were together he hadn't decided to do that.

HENRY PERCY

> He did it because you were proclaimed a traitor. But, my lord, he's gone now to Ravenspurgh, to help the Duke of Hereford, and he sent me to Berkeley to discover how large an army the Duke of York had there. Then he gave me orders to go on to Ravenspurgh.

NORTHUMBERLAND

> Have you forgotten who the Duke of Hereford is, boy?

HENRY PERCY

> No, my good lord, because I can't forget something I never remembered. I don't think I've ever seen him in my life.

NORTHUMBERLAND

> Then meet him now. This is the duke.

HENRY PERCY

> My gracious lord, I am in your service. I am young, but as I get older, I will demonstrate more impressive abilities.

HENRY BOLINGBROKE

> Thank you, kind Percy. I count myself happiest when remembering my good friends. I know that the reward for your love will be to witness how it helps me find greater success. My heart makes this promise to you, and this handshake seals that promise.

50   It shall be still thy true love's recompense.
     My heart this covenant makes, my hand thus seals it.

NORTHUMBERLAND
     How far is it to Berkeley? And what stir
     Keeps good old York there with his men of war?

HENRY PERCY
     There stands the castle, by yon tuft of trees,
55   Mann'd with three hundred men, as I have heard;
     And in it are the Lords of York, Berkeley, and Seymour;
     None else of name and noble estimate.

Enter LORD ROSS *and* LORD WILLOUGHBY

NORTHUMBERLAND
     Here come the Lords of Ross and Willoughby,
     Bloody with spurring, fiery-red with haste.

HENRY BOLINGBROKE
60   Welcome, my lords. I wot your love pursues
     A banish'd traitor. All my treasury
     Is yet but unfelt thanks, which more enrich'd
     Shall be your love and labor's recompense.

LORD ROSS
     Your presence makes us rich, most noble lord.

LORD WILLOUGHBY
65   And far surmounts our labor to attain it.

HENRY BOLINGBROKE
     Evermore thanks, the exchequer of the poor,
     Which, till my infant fortune comes to years,
     Stands for my bounty. But who comes here?

Enter LORD BERKELEY

NORTHUMBERLAND

How far is it to Berkeley? And what events keep good old
York there with his soldiers?

HENRY PERCY

There's the castle, over by that group of trees. I've heard
that it's protected by three hundred men, and that the
Lord of York, the Lord of Berkeley, and the Lord of
Seymour are there. There's no one else of title and noble
reputation inside.

LORD ROSS *and* LORD WILLOUGHBY *enter.*

NORTHUMBERLAND

Here come the Lord of Ross and the Lord of Willoughby.
They are bloody from sticking their spurs so hard into
their horses, and their faces are red from riding here so fast.

HENRY BOLINGBROKE

Welcome, my lords. I know that you've followed me here
out of love for me. Right now I can only pay you with my
thanks, but once I have money I'll repay your love and
hard work.

LORD ROSS

We are rich enough from just being here with you here,
most noble lord.

LORD WILLOUGHBY

And that richness is much more than anything we could
earn by working.

HENRY BOLINGBROKE

The poor earn their wealth in the form of gratitude. Until
my young fortune matures, that gratitude will have to
take the place of riches. But who's coming now?

LORD BERKELEY *enters.*

NORTHUMBERLAND
> It is my Lord of Berkeley, as I guess.

LORD BERKELEY
70 > My Lord of Hereford, my message is to you.

HENRY BOLINGBROKE
> My lord, my answer is—to Lancaster;
> And I am come to seek that name in England;
> And I must find that title in your tongue
> Before I make reply to aught you say.

LORD BERKELEY
75 > Mistake me not, my lord; 'tis not my meaning
> To raze one title of your honor out.
> To you, my lord, I come, what lord you will,
> From the most gracious regent of this land,
> The Duke of York, to know what pricks you on
80 > To take advantage of the absent time
> And fright our native peace with self-borne arms.

Enter DUKE OF YORK *attended*

HENRY BOLINGBROKE
> I shall not need transport my words by you.
> Here comes his grace in person. My noble uncle!

(He kneels.)

DUKE OF YORK
> Show me thy humble heart, and not thy knee,
85 > Whose duty is deceivable and false.

HENRY BOLINGBROKE
> My gracious uncle—

DUKE OF YORK
> Tut, tut!
> Grace me no grace, nor uncle me no uncle:
> I am no traitor's uncle; and that word "grace"
90 > In an ungracious mouth is but profane.
> Why have those banish'd and forbidden legs

NORTHUMBERLAND

> I think it's the Lord of Berkeley.

LORD BERKELEY

> Lord of Hereford, I have a message for you.

HENRY BOLINGBROKE

> My lord, I will answer only to my proper name, the Duke of Lancaster. And I have come to claim that name here in England. I must hear you call me that title before I respond to anything else you say.

LORD BERKELEY

> Don't misunderstand, my lord. It's not my intention to deny you your title. I've come to you, my lord—whatever title you want me to use—from the most gracious regent in this land, that is the Duke of York. I need to know what has led you to exploit the absence of our king and jeopardize the peace in this land with your armies.

The DUKE OF YORK and his assistants enter.

HENRY BOLINGBROKE

> (*to Lord Berkeley*) I won't have to pass my message through you. Here comes his grace in person. (*to the Duke of York*) My noble uncle!

>> (*He kneels.*)

DUKE OF YORK

> I don't want to see you kneeling. I know you don't really honor me.

HENRY BOLINGBROKE

> My gracious uncle—

DUKE OF YORK

> Tsk, tsk! Don't call me grace, and don't call me uncle. I am not the uncle of a traitor, and it's obscene to use that word "grace" when everybody knows you're ungracious. You were banished, so why have you come back to England? Why have you and your army marched miles

Dared once to touch a dust of England's ground?
But then more "why"? Why have they dared to march
So many miles upon her peaceful bosom,
95 Frighting her pale-faced villages with war
And ostentation of despised arms?
Comest thou because the anointed king is hence?
Why, foolish boy, the king is left behind
And in my loyal bosom lies his power.
100 Were I but now the lord of such hot youth
As when brave Gaunt, thy father, and myself
Rescued the Black Prince, that young Mars of men,
From forth the ranks of many thousand French,
O, then how quickly should this arm of mine.
105 Now prisoner to the palsy, chastise thee
And minister correction to thy fault!

HENRY BOLINGBROKE

My gracious uncle, let me know my fault.
On what condition stands it and wherein?

DUKE OF YORK

Even in condition of the worst degree,
110 In gross rebellion and detested treason.
Thou art a banish'd man, and here art come
Before the expiration of thy time,
In braving arms against thy sovereign.

HENRY BOLINGBROKE

As I was banish'd, I was banish'd Hereford;
115 But as I come, I come for Lancaster.
And, noble uncle, I beseech your grace
Look on my wrongs with an indifferent eye.
You are my father, for methinks in you
I see old Gaunt alive. O, then, my father,
120 Will you permit that I shall stand condemn'd
A wandering vagabond, my rights and royalties
Pluck'd from my arms perforce and given away
To upstart unthrifts? Wherefore was I born?
If that my cousin king be King of England,

across peaceful England, scaring villagers with threats
of war and displays of hateful weapons? Have you come
now because the king is away? Why, you foolish boy,
don't you know that the king has put me in charge while
he's away and that I am loyal to him? If I were still the
strong young man who, with your father, John of Gaunt,
rescued the king's father from thousands of French
soldiers, I would quickly smack you. But my arm is too
weak and shaky to administer punishment in that way.

HENRY BOLINGBROKE

My gracious uncle, why don't you tell me exactly what
I've done wrong?

DUKE OF YORK

You've done the worst that you can: rebellion and
treason. You are banished from this country and now
you've returned before you are allowed to do so. And
you've brought an army to fight against your king.

HENRY BOLINGBROKE

I was banished as Hereford, but I return as Lancaster.
And, noble uncle, I beg that you look at my missteps
impartially. I think I see my father in you. Oh, then, my
father, are you going to force me to be a wandering drifter
forever, while what is rightfully mine is taken away by
force and given to wasteful social climbers? Why was I
born? If my cousin is allowed to be the King of England,
then I must be allowed to be the Duke of Lancaster. You
have a son, Aumerle, who is my noble cousin. Let's say
that you died, and he had been treated this way. His uncle
Gaunt would have acted as a father to him and fought

125   It must be granted I am Duke of Lancaster.
        You have a son, Aumerle, my noble cousin.
        Had you first died, and he been thus trod down,
        He should have found his uncle Gaunt a father,
        To rouse his wrongs and chase them to the bay.
130   I am denied to sue my livery here,
        And yet my letters-patents give me leave.
        My father's goods are all distrain'd and sold,
        And these and all are all amiss employ'd.
        What would you have me do? I am a subject,
135   And I challenge law. Attorneys are denied me,
        And therefore, personally I lay my claim
        To my inheritance of free descent.

NORTHUMBERLAND
        The noble duke hath been too much abused.

LORD ROSS
        It stands your grace upon to do him right.

LORD WILLOUGHBY
140   Base men by his endowments are made great.

DUKE OF YORK
        My lords of England, let me tell you this:
        I have had feeling of my cousin's wrongs
        And labored all I could to do him right.
        But in this kind to come, in braving arms,
145   Be his own carver and cut out his way,
        To find out right with wrong, it may not be.
        And you that do abet him in this kind
        Cherish rebellion and are rebels all.

NORTHUMBERLAND
        The noble duke hath sworn his coming is
150   But for his own; and for the right of that
        We all have strongly sworn to give him aid.
        And let him ne'er see joy that breaks that oath!

DUKE OF YORK
        Well, well, I see the issue of these arms.
        I cannot mend it, I must needs confess,

to correct the wrongs done against him. I'm not allowed
to claim my inheritance, though I'm legally entitled to
do so. My father's possessions have all been wrongfully
confiscated and sold. What do you think I should do?
I am a subject of the King of England, aren't I? I claim
what is lawfully mine. Since I'm not allowed to have
attorneys, I must claim my inheritance myself.

NORTHUMBERLAND

The noble duke has been abused very much.

LORD ROSS

You owe it to him to treat him well.

LORD WILLOUGHBY

His money and property are making lowly men rich.

DUKE OF YORK

Listen, lords of England: I've known about the injustices
done to my cousin, and I have done everything I could
to correct them. But because of the way he's returned
to England, with an army and all these weapons, there's
nothing I can do. And you who are helping him are just
lowly rebels.

NORTHUMBERLAND

The noble duke has sworn he has come back to England
only for his own sake and not for any other reason. We
have all sworn to help him, and I hope anyone who breaks
that promise never feels joy again.

DUKE OF YORK

Well, well, I see how this is going to go. I admit I can't
change it, because my army is weak. But if God would

155 Because my power is weak and all ill left:
But if I could, by Him that gave me life,
I would attach you all and make you stoop
Unto the sovereign mercy of the king.
But since I cannot, be it known to you
160 I do remain as neuter. So, fare you well—
Unless you please to enter in the castle
And there repose you for this night.

HENRY BOLINGBROKE
An offer, uncle, that we will accept.
But we must win your grace to go with us
165 To Bristol Castle, which they say is held
By Bushy, Bagot, and their complices,
The caterpillars of the commonwealth,
Which I have sworn to weed and pluck away.

DUKE OF YORK
It may be I will go with you, but yet I'll pause,
170 For I am loath to break our country's laws.
Nor friends nor foes, to me welcome you are.
Things past redress are now with me past care.

Exeunt

let me, I'd arrest you all and make you stoop down before our king. But since I can't, I'm going to remain neutral. So, good luck to you. Or do you want to come sleep in the castle tonight?

HENRY BOLINGBROKE

Yes, uncle, we do. But first we must convince you to go with us to Bristol Castle, which I've heard is being held by Bushy, Bagot, and their accomplices. They are devouring the kingdom like caterpillars, and I've sworn to eliminate them.

DUKE OF YORK

I might go with you, but let me think about it first. I hate to break our country's laws. I look at you neither as a friend nor a foe, and I don't care about people's past misdeeds that can't be fixed now.

They exit.

ACT 2, SCENE 4

A camp in Wales. Enter EARL OF SALISBURY *and a*
WELSH CAPTAIN

CAPTAIN

My lord of Salisbury, we have stay'd ten days,
And hardly kept our countrymen together,
And yet we hear no tidings from the king;
Therefore we will disperse ourselves. Farewell.

EARL OF SALISBURY

5   Stay yet another day, thou trusty Welshman.
The king reposeth all his confidence in thee.

CAPTAIN

'Tis thought the king is dead. We will not stay.
The bay-trees in our country are all wither'd
And meteors fright the fixed stars of heaven;
10   The pale-faced moon looks bloody on the earth
And lean-look'd prophets whisper fearful change;
Rich men look sad and ruffians dance and leap,
The one in fear to lose what they enjoy,
The other to enjoy by rage and war.
15   These signs forerun the death or fall of kings.
Farewell. Our countrymen are gone and fled,
As well assured Richard their king is dead.

Exit

EARL OF SALISBURY

Ah, Richard! With the eyes of heavy mind
I see thy glory like a shooting star
20   Fall to the base earth from the firmament.
Thy sun sets weeping in the lowly west,
Witnessing storms to come, woe, and unrest.
Thy friends are fled to wait upon thy foes,
And crossly to thy good all fortune goes.

Exit

ACT 2, SCENE 4

A camp in Wales. The EARL OF SALISBURY *and a Welsh Captain enter.*

CAPTAIN

My lord of Salisbury, we've waited here for ten days and have had difficulty keeping our countrymen together. Since we've heard nothing from the king, we're going to leave. Good-bye.

EARL OF SALISBURY

My trusty Welshman, please stay one more day. The king has placed all his confidence in you.

CAPTAIN

It's believed that the king is dead, and we're not going to stay. The trees in our country are all withered, and there are meteors flashing in the sky and scaring the stars. The moon has turned red, and the fortune-tellers say that bad things are going to happen. Rich men suddenly look sad because they're afraid they're going to lose their possessions. And criminals are dancing because they know they're going to steal those possessions violently. All of these signs point to the death, or at least the fall, of kings. Good-bye. My countrymen have already fled, as they know that King Richard II is dead.

He exits.

EARL OF SALISBURY

Ah, Richard, I can see that your glory, like a shooting star, is falling from the sky to the ground, and the thought is weighing heavily on my mind. Your sun is setting in the west and it's crying, which tells me that storms of grief and chaos are coming. All of your friends have left you and pledged allegiance to your enemies, and fortune works against you.

He exits.

ACT THREE
SCENE 1

Bristol, before the castle. Enter HENRY BOLINGBROKE, DUKE
OF YORK, NORTHUMBERLAND, LORD ROSS, HENRY PERCY,
LORD WILLOUGHBY, *with* BUSHY *and* GREEN, *prisoners*

HENRY BOLINGBROKE

Bring forth these men.
Bushy and Green, I will not vex your souls—
Since presently your souls must part your bodies—
With too much urging your pernicious lives,
5   For 'twere no charity; yet, to wash your blood
From off my hands, here in the view of men
I will unfold some causes of your deaths.
You have misled a prince, a royal king,
A happy gentleman in blood and lineaments,
10   By you unhappied and disfigured clean.
You have in manner with your sinful hours
Made a divorce betwixt his queen and him,
Broke the possession of a royal bed
And stain'd the beauty of a fair queen's cheeks
15   With tears drawn from her eyes by your foul wrongs.
Myself, a prince by fortune of my birth,
Near to the king in blood, and near in love
Till you did make him misinterpret me,
Have stoop'd my neck under your injuries,
20   And sigh'd my English breath in foreign clouds,
Eating the bitter bread of banishment;
Whilst you have fed upon my signories,
Dispark'd my parks and fell'd my forest woods,
From my own windows torn my household coat,
25   Razed out my imprese, leaving me no sign,
Save men's opinions and my living blood,

ACT THREE

SCENE 1

In front of Bristol Castle. HENRY BOLINGBROKE, *the* DUKE
OF YORK, NORTHUMBERLAND, LORD ROSS, HENRY PERCY,
and LORD WILLOUGHBY, *escorting the prisoners* BUSHY *and*
GREEN, *enter.*

HENRY BOLINGBROKE

Bring these men to me. Bushy and Green, I won't
torment your souls with too much talk of your wicked
lives, since your souls will soon leave your bodies. But,
so no one may claim your execution was murder, I will
explain with these men as witnesses why you are legally
sentenced to death. You have deceived a king, a man
who was happy and attractive until you came along and
changed him. Through your evil ways, you have driven a
wedge between the king and the queen. You've interfered
with their happy marriage and caused the queen to suffer.
I, by the luck of my birth, am a prince. I am closely
related to the king, and until you changed his feelings
toward me, he loved me. Because of your actions, I've
had to live in exile in a foreign country, and meanwhile
you lived off my wealth and property here, leasing my
hunting grounds to others and cutting down my forests.
You tore my family's coat of arms out of the windows
of my house and destroyed all signs of my family's
existence. If not for men's opinions and the fact that I'm
still alive, no one would ever know that the property
was mine and that I am a member of the nobility. These
crimes and at least twice as many more condemn you
to death.

> *(He turns and addresses the others.)*

Make sure they are executed soon.

To show the world I am a gentleman.
This and much more, much more than twice all this,
Condemns you to the death. See them deliver'd over
30   To execution and the hand of death.

BUSHY

More welcome is the stroke of death to me
Than Bolingbroke to England. Lords, farewell.

GREEN

My comfort is that heaven will take our souls
And plague injustice with the pains of hell.

HENRY BOLINGBROKE

35   My Lord Northumberland, see them dispatch'd.

Exeunt **NORTHUMBERLAND** *and others, with the prisoners*

Uncle, you say the queen is at your house.
For God's sake, fairly let her be entreated.
Tell her I send to her my kind commends.
Take special care my greetings be deliver'd.

DUKE OF YORK

40   A gentleman of mine I have dispatch'd
With letters of your love to her at large.

HENRY BOLINGBROKE

Thank, gentle uncle. Come, lords, away.
To fight with Glendower and his complices.
Awhile to work, and after holiday.

Exeunt

BUSHY

> I welcome death more than I welcome the return of
> Bolingbroke to England. Lords, good-bye.

GREEN

> I am comforted knowing that our souls will go to heaven
> and that heaven will give hell to Bolingbroke, who
> committed this injustice.

HENRY BOLINGBROKE

> My lord Northumberland, see that they are killed.

NORTHUMBERLAND and others who are escorting the prisoners exit.

> Uncle, you said that the queen is at your house. For
> God's sake, let her be treated courteously. Give her my
> best, and make sure to deliver my greeting.

DUKE OF YORK

> I've sent a gentleman to her with the message.

HENRY BOLINGBROKE

> Thanks, kind uncle. Come, lords, let's leave. We've got to
> fight Glendower and his accomplices. First, we'll work,
> and then we'll be able to rest.

They exit.

ACT 3, SCENE 2

The coast of Wales. A castle in view. Drums; flourish and colors. Enter KING RICHARD II, *the* BISHOP OF CARLISLE, DUKE OF AUMERLE, *and Soldiers*

KING RICHARD II
Barkloughly castle call they this at hand?
DUKE OF AUMERLE
Yea, my lord. How brooks your grace the air
After your late tossing on the breaking seas?
KING RICHARD II
Needs must I like it well. I weep for joy
5   To stand upon my kingdom once again.
Dear earth, I do salute thee with my hand,
Though rebels wound thee with their horses' hoofs.
As a long-parted mother with her child
Plays fondly with her tears and smiles in meeting,
10   So, weeping, smiling, greet I thee, my earth,
And do thee favors with my royal hands.
Feed not thy sovereign's foe, my gentle earth,
Nor with thy sweets comfort his ravenous sense;
But let thy spiders, that suck up thy venom,
15   And heavy-gaited toads lie in their way,
Doing annoyance to the treacherous feet
Which with usurping steps do trample thee.
Yield stinging nettles to mine enemies;
And when they from thy bosom pluck a flower,
20   Guard it, I pray thee, with a lurking adder
Whose double tongue may with a mortal touch
Throw death upon thy sovereign's enemies.
Mock not my senseless conjuration, lords.
This earth shall have a feeling, and these stones
25   Prove armed soldiers, ere her native king
Shall falter under foul rebellion's arms.

ACT 3, SCENE 2

The coast of Wales. A castle is in view. Drums are played.
Trumpets blow. Military flags are carried onstage. KING
RICHARD II, *the* BISHOP OF CARLISLE, *the* DUKE OF
AUMERLE, *and some soldiers enter.*

KING RICHARD II
> Do they call this place Barkloughly Castle?

DUKE OF AUMERLE
> Yes, my lord. How do you like it here, after you've been
> tossing about on the open seas?

KING RICHARD II
> Of course I like it here. Standing here on my
> kingdom again makes me cry with joy. Dear earth,
> I salute you, even though insurgents are wounding
> you by riding their horses over you. Like a mother
> who has been away from her child for a long time,
> I cry and smile and greet you. Please, gentle earth,
> provide no nourishment or shelter for my enemies.
> Instead, let your venomous spiders and your toads
> get in their way. Put stinging **nettles** in their path.
> And when they pick a flower from the ground, let
> a poisonous snake bite and kill them. Lords, don't
> make fun of me for asking this. The earth will have
> feelings, and these stones will turn into armed
> soldiers, before I, England's legitimate king, let these
> terrible rebels defeat us.

*Plants with
jagged leaves
covered with
hairs that sting.*

BISHOP OF CARLISLE

> Fear not, my lord. That power that made you king
> Hath power to keep you king in spite of all.
> The means that heaven yields must be embraced,
> 30   And not neglected. Else, if heaven would,
> And we will not, heaven's offer we refuse,
> The proffer'd means of succor and redress.

DUKE OF AUMERLE

> He means, my lord, that we are too remiss
> Whilst Bolingbroke, through our security,
> 35   Grows strong and great in substance and in power.

KING RICHARD II

> Discomfortable cousin! Know'st thou not
> That when the searching eye of heaven is hid
> Behind the globe, that lights the lower world,
> Then thieves and robbers range abroad unseen
> 40   In murders and in outrage, boldly here?
> But when from under this terrestrial ball
> He fires the proud tops of the eastern pines
> And darts his light through every guilty hole,
> Then murders, treasons, and detested sins,
> 45   The cloak of night being pluck'd from off their backs,
> Stand bare and naked, trembling at themselves.
> So when this thief, this traitor, Bolingbroke,
> Who all this while hath revell'd in the night
> Whilst we were wandering with the antipodes,
> 50   Shall see us rising in our throne, the east,
> His treasons will sit blushing in his face,
> Not able to endure the sight of day,
> But self-affrighted tremble at his sin.
> Not all the water in the rough rude sea
> 55   Can wash the balm off from an anointed king.
> The breath of worldly men cannot depose
> The deputy elected by the Lord.
> For every man that Bolingbroke hath press'd
> To lift shrewd steel against our golden crown,

BISHOP OF CARLISLE

> Don't worry, my lord, the power that made you king
> is the same power that will keep you king in spite of all
> these troubles. We must embrace the opportunities that
> God gives us and not neglect them. Otherwise, we're
> rejecting both God's protection from these problems as
> well as his solution for them.

DUKE OF AUMERLE

> What he means, my lord, is that we're being neglectful
> because of overconfidence, while Bolingbroke is
> growing stronger.

KING RICHARD II

> You are so discouraging, cousin! Don't you know that at
> nighttime, when the sun has set, thieves roam the earth
> unseen, boldly committing murder and other crimes? But
> when the sun comes up and lights the treetops and every
> dark hole, then those same criminals stand trembling
> with no way to hide. So when this thief, this traitor
> Bolingbroke, who has been committing all these crimes
> during the nighttime, sees us coming up with the sun,
> he'll be ashamed and will tremble at the light of day. All
> the water in an ocean can't wash away a king's right to the
> throne. Mere mortals can't get rid of someone who has
> been appointed by God. For every solider Bolingbroke
> has enlisted to fight against me, God has given me an
> angel. And when angels fight, the weak men fall, since
> heaven always guards those who are right.

60   God for his Richard hath in heavenly pay
        A glorious angel. Then, if angels fight,
        Weak men must fall, for heaven still guards the right.

        Enter EARL OF SALISBURY

        Welcome, my lord. How far off lies your power?

EARL OF SALISBURY

        Nor near nor farther off, my gracious lord,
65   Than this weak arm. Discomfort guides my tongue
        And bids me speak of nothing but despair.
        One day too late, I fear me, noble lord,
        Hath clouded all thy happy days on earth.
        O, call back yesterday, bid time return,
70   And thou shalt have twelve thousand fighting men!
        Today, today, unhappy day, too late,
        O'erthrows thy joys, friends, fortune, and thy state:
        For all the Welshmen, hearing thou wert dead.
        Are gone to Bolingbroke, dispersed and fled.

DUKE OF AUMERLE

75   Comfort, my liege. Why looks your grace so pale?

KING RICHARD II

        But now the blood of twenty thousand men
        Did triumph in my face, and they are fled;
        And, till so much blood thither come again,
        Have I not reason to look pale and dead?
80   All souls that will be safe fly from my side,
        For time hath set a blot upon my pride.

DUKE OF AUMERLE

        Comfort, my liege. Remember who you are.

KING RICHARD II

        I had forgot myself. Am I not king?
        Awake, thou coward majesty! Thou sleepest.
85   Is not the king's name twenty thousand names?
        Arm, arm, my name! A puny subject strikes
        At thy great glory. Look not to the ground,

EARL OF SALISBURY *enters.*

Welcome, my lord. How far away is your army?

EARL OF SALISBURY

My army consists only of me, and I am too upset to talk
of anything but despair. We are one day too late and have
lost our chance of seeing happy times again. Oh, I wish
it were still yesterday. If we could go back in time, we'd
have twelve thousand men ready to fight on our side!
Today, today—it is an unhappy day. Today has taken
away any chance for joy, friends, wealth, and power. All
the Welshmen heard that you were dead, and they've all
joined Bolingbroke's army.

DUKE OF AUMERLE

Cheer up, my lord. Why are you so pale?

KING RICHARD II

Only a moment ago, I had twenty thousand men fighting
for me, and now they've all fled. Until they return, aren't
I allowed to look as pale as if I were dead? Anyone who
wants to be safe flees from me, as recent events have
tarnished my reputation.

DUKE OF AUMERLE

Cheer up, my lord. Don't forget that you're the king.

KING RICHARD II

I forgot. I'm the king, aren't I? Awake, you cowardly
king. You're sleeping. Isn't being the king worth as much
as twenty thousand men? Prepare for action, my name!
A young and weak subject is trying to damage your
glory. Don't hang your head low. You favorite men of the

Ye favorites of a king. Are we not high?
High be our thoughts: I know my uncle York
90   Hath power enough to serve our turn. But who
       comes here?

Enter SIR STEPHEN SCROOP

SIR STEPHEN SCROOP
    More health and happiness betide my liege
    Than can my care-tuned tongue deliver him!
KING RICHARD II
    Mine ear is open and my heart prepared.
    The worst is worldly loss thou canst unfold.
95   Say, is my kingdom lost? Why, 'twas my care
    And what loss is it to be rid of care?
    Strives Bolingbroke to be as great as we?
    Greater he shall not be. If he serve God,
    We'll serve Him too and be his fellow so.
100   Revolt our subjects? That we cannot mend.
    They break their faith to God as well as us.
    Cry woe, destruction, ruin, and decay:
    The worst is death, and death will have his day.
SIR STEPHEN SCROOP
    Glad am I that your highness is so arm'd
105   To bear the tidings of calamity.
    Like an unseasonable stormy day
    Which makes the silver rivers drown their shores,
    As if the world were all dissolved to tears,
    So high above his limits swells the rage
110   Of Bolingbroke, covering your fearful land
    With hard bright steel and hearts harder than steel.
    Whitebeards have arm'd their thin and hairless scalps
    Against thy majesty; boys, with women's voices,
    Strive to speak big and clap their female joints
115   In stiff unwieldy arms against thy crown:
    The very beadsmen learn to bend their bows

king—aren't we high above them all? Then we should aim high as well: I know my uncle York has enough troops for our needs. But who's coming now?

SIR STEPHEN SCROOP *enters.*

SIR STEPHEN SCROOP

I hope more health and happiness come to you, my lord, than my grief-stricken tongue can offer.

KING RICHARD II

My ears are open, and my heart is ready. The worst you can tell me about are losses for me here on earth. So, did I lose my kingdom? It was my problem, and what loss is it to be rid of a problem? Is Bolingbroke still trying to overthrow me? If he serves God, we will serve God, too, and then the two of us will be merely equals. Are our subjects revolting? We can't fix that. They break their faith with God as well as with us. Though you may cry out about woe, destruction, ruin, and decay, death is the worst fate of all, and the time for death will come.

SIR STEPHEN SCROOP

I'm glad that your highness is prepared for the worst. Bolingbroke is bursting with rage and his army is attacking all across England. It's like an unexpected flood that makes it seem like the world is crying. Even old men with white beards have joined forces against your majesty, and young boys whose voices have not yet deepened to manhood. The men whom we paid to pray for us are also now on their side, and women are fighting against you as well. Everything is going far worse for you than I can possibly describe.

Of double-fatal yew against thy state;
Yea, distaff-women manage rusty bills
Against thy seat. Both young and old rebel,
120   And all goes worse than I have power to tell.

KING RICHARD II

Too well, too well thou tell'st a tale so ill.
Where is the Earl of Wiltshire? Where is Bagot?
What is become of Bushy? Where is Green?
That they have let the dangerous enemy
125   Measure our confines with such peaceful steps?
If we prevail, their heads shall pay for it.
I warrant they have made peace with Bolingbroke.

SIR STEPHEN SCROOP

Peace have they made with him indeed, my lord.

KING RICHARD II

O villains, vipers, damn'd without redemption!
130   Dogs, easily won to fawn on any man!
Snakes, in my heart-blood warm'd, that sting my heart!
Three Judases, each one thrice worse than Judas!
Would they make peace? Terrible hell
Make war upon their spotted souls for this!

SIR STEPHEN SCROOP

135   Sweet love, I see, changing his property,
Turns to the sourest and most deadly hate.
Again uncurse their souls. Their peace is made
With heads and not with hands. Those whom you curse
Have felt the worst of death's destroying wound
140   And lie full low, graved in the hollow ground.

DUKE OF AUMERLE

Is Bushy, Green, and the Earl of Wiltshire dead?

SIR STEPHEN SCROOP

Ay, all of them at Bristol lost their heads.

DUKE OF AUMERLE

Where is the duke my father with his power?

KING RICHARD II

You are describing these horrible things too vividly.
Where is the Earl of Wiltshire? Where is Bagot? What
happened to Bushy? Where is Green? They didn't let
the dangerous enemy cross over our territories without
any opposition, did they? If we win, they'll pay for their
failures with their heads. I'll bet they've made peace
with Bolingbroke.

SIR STEPHEN SCROOP

Oh, yes, they've made peace, my lord.

KING RICHARD II

Oh, they are villains and vipers, damned without any
hope for redemption! They're like dogs that will suck
up to anyone! They're three **Judases**, but each three
times worse than Judas! I hope their guilt-stained
souls are punished terribly for what they've done!

Judas was the disciple who betrayed Jesus to Jewish authorities in return for thirty pieces of silver.

SIR STEPHEN SCROOP

I see how your love turns into the deadliest of hatred.
Please, take back your curses. Their peace wasn't made
by joining forces with Bolingbroke. It was made with
God, when they were executed. They are all in their
graves now.

DUKE OF AUMERLE

Are Bushy, Green, and the Earl of Wiltshire dead?

SIR STEPHEN SCROOP

Yes, they were all beheaded at Bristol.

DUKE OF AUMERLE

Where is my father with his army?

KING RICHARD II

No matter where. Of comfort no man speak.
145 Let's talk of graves, of worms, and epitaphs;
Make dust our paper and with rainy eyes
Write sorrow on the bosom of the earth.
Let's choose executors and talk of wills.
And yet not so, for what can we bequeath
150 Save our deposed bodies to the ground?
Our lands, our lives, and all are Bolingbroke's,
And nothing can we call our own but death
And that small model of the barren earth
Which serves as paste and cover to our bones.
155 For God's sake, let us sit upon the ground
And tell sad stories of the death of kings—
How some have been deposed; some slain in war,
Some haunted by the ghosts they have deposed;
Some poison'd by their wives: some sleeping kill'd;
160 All murder'd. For within the hollow crown
That rounds the mortal temples of a king
Keeps Death his court, and there the antic sits,
Scoffing his state and grinning at his pomp,
Allowing him a breath, a little scene,
165 To monarchize, be fear'd and kill with looks,
Infusing him with self and vain conceit,
As if this flesh which walls about our life
Were brass impregnable, and humor'd thus
Comes at the last and with a little pin
170 Bores through his castle wall, and farewell, king!
Cover your heads and mock not flesh and blood
With solemn reverence. Throw away respect,
Tradition, form, and ceremonious duty,
For you have but mistook me all this while.
175 I live with bread like you, feel want,
Taste grief, need friends. Subjected thus,
How can you say to me, I am a king?

KING RICHARD II

It doesn't matter where he is. Let's not try to cheer ourselves up. We must talk about graves and worms and **epitaphs**. We'll make the dust our paper and use our tears to write a message of sorrow on the earth. Let's choose our **executors** and talk of wills. And, yet, what can we bequeath to anyone other than leaving our rotting bodies to the ground? Our lands and our lives now belong to Bolingbroke, and we can call nothing our own except for our deaths and that little patch of earth that will cover our buried bodies. For God's sake, let's sit on the ground and tell sad stories of the death of kings, how some were overthrown and others killed in war. Some were haunted by the ghosts of the kings they had overthrown. Still others were poisoned by their wives, while others were killed in their sleep. All of them, however, were murdered. There is always death around kings, and there's no way to escape it. Death laughs at the king's reign and mocks his great ceremonies, allowing him to live a little while and play the monarch. Death fills him with pride as if the king's body were immortal, and at the end death comes and with little effort kills the body. Then good-bye, king! So stop treating me so respectfully. There's no need to pretend that I am any different than you. You've been wrong about me all this time. I feel all the same things that you do. I have desires and feel sad and need friends, just like you. How, then, can you say that I'm a king?

Inscriptions on tombstones.

People appointed by others to carry out the terms of their wills.

BISHOP OF CARLISLE

My lord, wise men ne'er sit and wail their woes,
But presently prevent the ways to wail.
180   To fear the foe, since fear oppresseth strength,
Gives in your weakness strength unto your foe,
And so your follies fight against yourself.
Fear and be slain—no worse can come to fight:
And fight and die is death destroying death,
185   Where fearing dying pays death servile breath.

DUKE OF AUMERLE

My father hath a power. Inquire of him
And learn to make a body of a limb.

KING RICHARD II

Thou chidest me well. Proud Bolingbroke, I come
To change blows with thee for our day of doom.
190   This ague fit of fear is overblown.
An easy task it is to win our own.
Say, Scroop, where lies our uncle with his power?
Speak sweetly, man, although thy looks be sour.

SIR STEPHEN SCROOP

Men judge by the complexion of the sky
195   The state and inclination of the day:
So may you by my dull and heavy eye,
My tongue hath but a heavier tale to say.
I play the torturer, by small and small
To lengthen out the worst that must be spoken.
200   Your uncle York is join'd with Bolingbroke,
And all your northern castles yielded up,
And all your southern gentlemen in arms
Upon his party.

KING RICHARD II

Thou hast said enough.
205   (*to* DUKE OF AUMERLE) Beshrew thee, cousin, which didst
lead me forth
Of that sweet way I was in to despair!
What say you now? What comfort have we now?

BISHOP OF CARLISLE

My lord, wise men never sit and feel sorry for themselves
but try to fix the causes of their sorrow. Since fear
weakens you, fearing your enemy only works against
you and helps your enemy. If you're scared that you'll
die, well, that's the worst that can happen in battle. But
fighting and dying is a way of beating death, because then
you die nobly. But being scared and dying gives death
the victory.

DUKE OF AUMERLE

My father has soldiers. Let's figure out where he is and
make an army out of the men he has.

KING RICHARD II

Your scolding does me good. Proud Bolingbroke, I'll
exchange blows with you on our day of destiny. My fit of
fear has passed. It should be easy to get our men together.
Scroop, where is my uncle with his men? Tell me good
news, man, even though you look bad.

SIR STEPHEN SCROOP

Men often determine what the day is going to be like
by looking at the sky, so you should know by my dull
and gloomy eyes that I'm about to deliver bad news.
I'm acting like a torturer, drawing out the pain of what
I have to say. Your uncle York has joined forces with
Bolingbroke. They have possession of all your northern
castles now, and all your men of rank in the south are
fighting for them, too.

KING RICHARD II

You have said enough. (*to the Duke of Aumerle*) I curse
you, cousin, for convincing me not to be sad anymore.
What do you have to say now? What comforts us now?
I swear to God, I will forever hate the man who tells me
not to despair now. Go to Flint Castle. That's where I will

By heaven, I'll hate him everlastingly
That bids me be of comfort any more.
210   Go to Flint castle. There I'll pine away;
A king, woe's slave, shall kingly woe obey.
That power I have, discharge; and let them go
To ear the land that hath some hope to grow,
For I have none. Let no man speak again
215   To alter this, for counsel is but vain.

DUKE OF AUMERLE

My liege, one word.

KING RICHARD II

                    He does me double wrong
That wounds me with the flatteries of his tongue.
Discharge my followers. Let them hence away,
220   From Richard's night to Bolingbroke's fair day.

Exeunt

wait. I am a king, but I am a slave of sorrow, and I will follow sorrow's orders. Tell my army that they may leave and go work for some cause that has hope, since I have none. I don't want to hear anyone trying to change my mind. Any advice is pointless.

DUKE OF AUMERLE

My lord, may I have a word?

KING RICHARD II

The person who tries to convince me again not to despair will become the second person to treat me poorly. Let my army go. England will be Bolingbroke's very soon.

They exit.

ACT 3, SCENE 3

Wales. Before Flint castle. Enter, with drum and colors,
HENRY BOLINGBROKE, DUKE OF YORK, NORTHUMBERLAND,
Attendants, and forces

HENRY BOLINGBROKE
So that by this intelligence we learn
The Welshmen are dispersed, and Salisbury
Is gone to meet the king, who lately landed
With some few private friends upon this coast.

NORTHUMBERLAND
5   The news is very fair and good, my lord:
Richard not far from hence hath hid his head.

DUKE OF YORK
It would beseem the Lord Northumberland
To say "King Richard." Alack the heavy day
When such a sacred king should hide his head!

NORTHUMBERLAND
10   Your grace mistakes; only to be brief
Left I his title out.

DUKE OF YORK
                    The time hath been,
Would you have been so brief with him, he would
Have been so brief with you, to shorten you,
15   For taking so the head, your whole head's length.

HENRY BOLINGBROKE
Mistake not, uncle, further than you should.

DUKE OF YORK
Take not, good cousin, further than you should.
Lest you mistake the heavens are o'er our heads.

HENRY BOLINGBROKE
I know it, uncle, and oppose not myself
20   Against their will. But who comes here?

ACT 3, SCENE 3

Wales, outside Flint Castle. HENRY BOLINGBROKE, DUKE
OF YORK, *and* NORTHUMBERLAND *enter, with ceremonial
flags and drums sounding. Several attendants and soldiers
accompany them.*

HENRY BOLINGBROKE

So we know from this latest news that the Welshmen have
left the battlefield and that the king has landed with some
of his friends on the coast, where Salisbury has gone to
meet him.

NORTHUMBERLAND

It's good news, my lord. Richard is hiding not very far
from here.

DUKE OF YORK

It would be better for Lord Northumberland to call him
"King Richard." We should mourn the day that a king
has to hide.

NORTHUMBERLAND

Your grace misunderstands me. I only left off his title for
the sake of brevity.

DUKE OF YORK

There was a time when, if you'd been so brief in his
presence, he would have made you even briefer, by
chopping off your head.

HENRY BOLINGBROKE

Uncle, don't take this misunderstanding too far.

DUKE OF YORK

Good cousin, don't take more than you should, or you
may forget heaven rules over us.

HENRY BOLINGBROKE

I know it, uncle, and won't oppose the will of heaven. But
who is coming?

Enter HENRY PERCY

Welcome, Harry: what, will not this castle yield?

HENRY PERCY

The castle royally is mann'd, my lord,
Against thy entrance.

HENRY BOLINGBROKE

Royally!
25   Why, it contains no king?

HENRY PERCY

Yes, my good lord,
It doth contain a king. King Richard lies
Within the limits of yon lime and stone;
And with him are the Lord Aumerle, Lord Salisbury,
30   Sir Stephen Scroop, besides a clergyman
Of holy reverence—who, I cannot learn.

NORTHUMBERLAND

O, belike it is the Bishop of Carlisle.

HENRY BOLINGBROKE

Noble lords,
Go to the rude ribs of that ancient castle;
35   Through brazen trumpet send the breath of parley
Into his ruin'd ears, and thus deliver:
Henry Bolingbroke
On both his knees doth kiss King Richard's hand
And sends allegiance and true faith of heart
40   To his most royal person, hither come
Even at his feet to lay my arms and power,
Provided that my banishment repeal'd
And lands restored again be freely granted.
If not, I'll use the advantage of my power
45   And lay the summer's dust with showers of blood
Rain'd from the wounds of slaughter'd Englishmen:
The which, how far off from the mind of Bolingbroke
It is, such crimson tempest should bedrench
The fresh green lap of fair King Richard's land,

HENRY PERCY *enters.*

Welcome, Harry. What, won't this castle give in?

HENRY PERCY

The castle is guarded by royal soldiers, my lord, and they won't let you enter.

HENRY BOLINGBROKE

Royal! But there's no king here, is there?

HENRY PERCY

Yes, my lord, there is a king here. King Richard is inside, along with Lord Aumerle, Lord Salisbury, Sir Stephen Scroop, as well a holy clergyman whom I don't know.

NORTHUMBERLAND

It's probably the Bishop of Carlisle.

HENRY BOLINGBROKE

Noble lords, approach the crude walls of this old castle and let the trumpets sound a signal to the king that we want to meet. Deliver this message: Henry Bolingbroke kneels before King Richard, kisses his hand, and offers his loyalty and true faith of heart. I come to lay my weapons and my power at his feet, as long as he repeals my banishment and freely gives back all my lands. If he won't, I'll use my power to rain his Englishmen's blood on the summer's dust. By kneeling submissively before him I'll show how little I desire to drench his green lands in this way. Go, tell him, and meanwhile we'll march here on the plain. Let's march without the drums so that they can clearly see our excellent military equipment from the castle's ruined roof. I think King Richard and I should meet in the same way that lightning and rain mix in the sky, producing thunder that rips it apart. If he's the lightning, I'll be the rain. He can rage, while I will yield

50 My stooping duty tenderly shall show.
Go, signify as much, while here we march
Upon the grassy carpet of this plain.
Let's march without the noise of threatening drum,
That from this castle's tatter'd battlements
55 Our fair appointments may be well perused.
Methinks King Richard and myself should meet
With no less terror than the elements
Of fire and water, when their thundering shock
At meeting tears the cloudy cheeks of heaven.
60 Be he the fire; I'll be the yielding water.
The rage be his, whilst on the earth I rain
My waters—on the earth, and not on him.
March on, and mark King Richard how he looks.

*Parle without, and answer within. Then a flourish. Enter on
the walls,* KING RICHARD II, *the* BISHOP OF CARLISLE, DUKE
OF AUMERLE, SIR STEPHEN SCROOP, *and* EARL OF SALISBURY

See, see, King Richard doth himself appear,
65 As doth the blushing discontented sun
From out the fiery portal of the east,
When he perceives the envious clouds are bent
To dim his glory and to stain the track
Of his bright passage to the occident.

DUKE OF YORK

70 Yet looks he like a king. Behold, his eye,
As bright as is the eagle's, lightens forth
Controlling majesty. Alack, alack, for woe,
That any harm should stain so fair a show!

KING RICHARD II

(*to* NORTHUMBERLAND) We are amazed; and thus long
have we stood
75 To watch the fearful bending of thy knee,
Because we thought ourself thy lawful king:
And if we be, how dare thy joints forget

and pour my waters on the earth. But only on the earth, not on him. March along, and notice how King Richard looks.

They call from outside for a meeting, and someone answers from within. Trumpets blow. KING RICHARD II, *the* BISHOP OF CARLISLE, DUKE OF AUMERLE, SIR STEPHEN SCROOP, *and* EARL OF SALISBURY *appear on the walls of the castle.*

See, King Richard himself appears, just as the sun rises unhappily in the east when it sees the clouds covering the sky and trying to hide his rays.

DUKE OF YORK

He still looks like a king. Look, his eye is as bright as an eagle's and commands authority. It would be a shame to harm his fair appearance!

KING RICHARD II

(*to* NORTHUMBERLAND) I am astonished that I've stood here waiting so long and you haven't yet kneeled, since I thought I was still your lawful king. And if I am, how dare you not kneel in my presence? If I am not, prove to me that God has dismissed me from my position. No

To pay their awful duty to our presence?
If we be not, show us the hand of God
80   That hath dismissed us from our stewardship;
For well we know, no hand of blood and bone
Can grip the sacred handle of our scepter,
Unless he do profane, steal, or usurp.
And though you think that all, as you have done,
85   Have torn their souls by turning them from us,
And we are barren and bereft of friends;
Yet know, my master, God omnipotent,
Is mustering in his clouds on our behalf
Armies of pestilence; and they shall strike
90   Your children yet unborn and unbegot,
That lift your vassal hands against my head
And threat the glory of my precious crown.
Tell Bolingbroke—for yon methinks he stands—
That every stride he makes upon my land
95   Is dangerous treason. He is come to open
The purple testament of bleeding war;
But ere the crown he looks for live in peace,
Ten thousand bloody crowns of mothers' sons
Shall ill become the flower of England's face,
100   Change the complexion of her maid-pale peace
To scarlet indignation and bedew
Her pastures' grass with faithful English blood.

NORTHUMBERLAND

The king of heaven forbid our lord the king
Should so with civil and uncivil arms
105   Be rush'd upon! Thy thrice-noble cousin,
Harry Bolingbroke, doth humbly kiss thy hand;
And by the honorable tomb he swears,
That stands upon your royal grandsire's bones,
And by the royalties of both your bloods,
110   Currents that spring from one most gracious head,
And by the buried hand of warlike Gaunt,
And by the worth and honor of himself,

mortal man, after all, can take away my scepter, unless he steals it or usurps it against the will of God. Even if you think that, like you, everyone has put their souls in danger by turning away from me, and that I have no friends, you should know that God, my master, is gathering disease and agony in his clouds on my behalf. They will strike the unborn children of anyone who raises their hands against me and the glory of my crown. Tell Bolingbroke—for I think he's standing over there—that every step he takes on my land is a dangerous act of treason. He has come to wage war against me. But ten thousand sons will die, faithful Englishman's blood will stain the pastures, and peace will turn to anger before he ever gets the crown he seeks.

NORTHUMBERLAND

God forbid that anyone would attack the king! Your noble cousin Harry Bolingbroke kisses your hand. He swears by your grandfather's grave, by the royal blood you share, by the buried hand of his father Gaunt, and by his own honor that he has no intention of doing anything but kneeling down and asking for his land and money back. Once you've given him that, he'll commit to never use his weapons, to put his warhorses in stables, and to dedicate himself to your faithful service. He swears that this is fair to him as a prince. I, as a gentleman, believe him.

Comprising all that may be sworn or said,
His coming hither hath no further scope
115   Than for his lineal royalties and to beg
Enfranchisement immediate on his knees:
Which on thy royal party granted once,
His glittering arms he will commend to rust,
His barbed steeds to stables, and his heart
120   To faithful service of your majesty.
This swears he, as he is a prince, is just;
And, as I am a gentleman, I credit him.

KING RICHARD II

Northumberland, say thus the king returns:
His noble cousin is right welcome hither;
125   And all the number of his fair demands
Shall be accomplish'd without contradiction.
With all the gracious utterance thou hast
Speak to his gentle hearing kind commends.
(to DUKE OF AUMERLE) We do debase ourselves, cousin,
      do we not,
130   To look so poorly and to speak so fair?
Shall we call back Northumberland, and send
Defiance to the traitor, and so die?

DUKE OF AUMERLE

No, good my lord; let's fight with gentle words
Till time lend friends and friends their helpful swords.

KING RICHARD II

135   O God! O God, that e'er this tongue of mine,
That laid the sentence of dread banishment
On yon proud man, should take it off again
With words of sooth! O that I were as great
As is my grief, or lesser than my name!
140   Or that I could forget what I have been,
Or not remember what I must be now!
Swell'st thou, proud heart? I'll give thee scope to beat,
Since foes have scope to beat both thee and me.

KING RICHARD II

Northumberland, tell him the king says that his noble
cousin is welcome here. His demands are fair, and all of
them will be done as he requests. With as much grace
as you can, send him my kind greetings. (*to the* DUKE
OF AUMERLE) Cousin, aren't I dishonoring myself by
looking so wretched and speaking so kindly? Should I call
back Northumberland and tell him to send only words
of defiance to the traitor—and in doing so ensure that
Bolingbroke's army will kill me?

DUKE OF AUMERLE

No, my good lord. Let's do battle with gentle words until
we've had time to gather our friends and their weapons.

KING RICHARD II

Oh, God! It's unbelievable that after sentencing
that proud man to banishment, I would now lift his
punishment with soothing words! I wish that I were as
great as I am a sad, or that I weren't a king. I wish I could
forget that I've been a king, and that I must act like a
king now. Is my heart beating faster? I'll let it beat faster,
since my enemies have the ability to beat both my heart
and me.

DUKE OF AUMERLE
>Northumberland comes back from Bolingbroke.

KING RICHARD II
145 What must the king do now? Must he submit?
The king shall do it. Must he be deposed?
The king shall be contented. Must he lose
The name of king? I' God's name, let it go.
I'll give my jewels for a set of beads,
150 My gorgeous palace for a hermitage,
My gay apparel for an almsman's gown,
My figured goblets for a dish of wood,
My scepter for a palmer's walking staff,
My subjects for a pair of carved saints
155 And my large kingdom for a little grave,
A little little grave, an obscure grave;
Or I'll be buried in the king's highway,
Some way of common trade, where subjects' feet
May hourly trample on their sovereign's head;
160 For on my heart they tread now whilst I live;
And buried once, why not upon my head?
Aumerle, thou weep'st, my tender-hearted cousin!
We'll make foul weather with despised tears;
Our sighs and they shall lodge the summer corn,
165 And make a dearth in this revolting land.
Or shall we play the wantons with our woes,
And make some pretty match with shedding tears?
As thus, to drop them still upon one place,
Till they have fretted us a pair of graves
170 Within the earth; and, therein laid—there lies
Two kinsmen digg'd their graves with weeping eyes.
Would not this ill do well? Well, well, I see
I talk but idly, and you laugh at me.
Most mighty prince, my Lord Northumberland,
175 What says King Bolingbroke? Will his majesty
Give Richard leave to live till Richard die?
You make a leg, and Bolingbroke says ay.

DUKE OF AUMERLE

> Northumberland is coming back from speaking to
> Bolingbroke.

KING RICHARD II

> What must the king do now? Must the king surrender?
> He will do it. Must the king be overthrown? He will
> be happy. Must the king no longer be called king? In
> God's name, he'll renounce it. I'll trade my jewels for
> a rosary, my gorgeous palace for a hermit's dwelling,
> my nice clothes for a beggar's shirt, my ornamented
> cups for a wooden dish, my scepter for a pilgrim's cane,
> my subjects for a pair of carved saints, and trade my
> kingdom for a small and unmarked grave. Or bury me in
> a busy highway, where my subjects can trample my head
> constantly, since they are trampling my heart now while
> I'm still alive. Once I'm buried, why not trample on my
> head? Aumerle, my softhearted cousin, you are crying.
> We'll use our tears to create violent storms, and with our
> sighs they will beat down the crops and cause famine in
> this rebellious land. Or shall we play with our woes and
> devise some clever game with our tears? We could keep
> them falling continually in one spot until they've carved
> us a pair of graves in the earth. We'd lie in the graves,
> and the tombstone would say "There lie two relatives
> who dug their graves with tears." Wouldn't that be a
> good game to play? Well, well, I speak foolishly, and you
> are laughing at me. My lord Northumberland, mighty
> prince, what does King Bolingbroke say? Will his majesty
> allow me to live until I die? You bow, and Bolingbroke
> decides.

NORTHUMBERLAND
>   My lord, in the base court he doth attend
>   To speak with you; may it please you to come down.

KING RICHARD II
180   Down, down I come, like glistering Phaethon,
>   Wanting the manage of unruly jades.
>   In the base court? Base court, where kings grow base,
>   To come at traitors' calls and do them grace.
>   In the base court? Come down? Down, court!
>   Down, king!
185   For night owls shriek where mounting larks should sing.

Exeunt from above

HENRY BOLINGBROKE
>   What says his majesty?

NORTHUMBERLAND
>   Sorrow and grief of heart
>   Makes him speak fondly, like a frantic man
>   Yet he is come.

Enter **KING RICHARD** *and his attendants below*

HENRY BOLINGBROKE
190   Stand all apart,
>   And show fair duty to his majesty.

(He kneels down.)

>   My gracious lord—

KING RICHARD II
>   Fair cousin, you debase your princely knee
>   To make the base earth proud with kissing it.
195   Me rather had my heart might feel your love
>   Than my unpleased eye see your courtesy.
>   Up, cousin, up! Your heart is up, I know,
>   Thus high at least, although your knee be low.

NORTHUMBERLAND

> My lord, he waits in the outer court below to speak with
> you. Will you come down?

KING RICHARD II

> I'm coming down, like shining **Phaeton**, unable
> to control unruly horses. In the bottom court? The
> bottom court, where kings become common enough
> to obey a traitor's summons and bow to them. In
> the bottom court? Come down? The bottom court!
> And now the king is on the bottom! Everything is
> backward, and night owls shriek when mounting
> larks should be singing.

Son of Helios, the sun god, in Greek myth. Helios allowed him to drive the chariot of the sun, but Phaeton was unable to control the horses pulling the chariot. They veered too close to the earth, burning it, until Zeus struck Phaeton down with a thunderbolt.

They exit from above.

HENRY BOLINGBROKE

> What does the king say?

NORTHUMBERLAND

> His sorrow makes him speak foolishly, like a mad man.
> But he's coming.

KING RICHARD *and his attendants enter below.*

HENRY BOLINGBROKE

> Stand apart, and show your duty to the king.

(He kneels.)

> My gracious lord.

KING RICHARD II

> Fair cousin, you insult your princely knee by touching
> it to the lowly earth. I'd rather my heart feel your love
> than my eyes see your fake courtesy. Get up, cousin. Your
> heart is proud, I know, even if your knee is humbled.

HENRY BOLINGBROKE
> My gracious lord, I come but for mine own.

KING RICHARD II
200 > Your own is yours, and I am yours, and all.

HENRY BOLINGBROKE
> So far be mine, my most redoubted lord,
> As my true service shall deserve your love.

KING RICHARD II
> Well you deserve. They well deserve to have,
> That know the strong'st and surest way to get.
205 > Uncle, give me your hands. Nay, dry your eyes.
> Tears show their love but want their remedies.
> Cousin, I am too young to be your father,
> Though you are old enough to be my heir.
> What you will have, I'll give, and willing too;
210 > For do we must what force will have us do.
> Set on towards London, cousin, is it so?

HENRY BOLINGBROKE
> Yea, my good lord.

KING RICHARD II
> Then I must not say no.

Flourish. Exeunt

HENRY BOLINGBROKE

> My gracious lord, I'm only here to reclaim my own property.

KING RICHARD II

> Your property is yours, and I am your king.

HENRY BOLINGBROKE

> My dreaded lord, you are my king only if I deserve your love.

KING RICHARD II

> You deserve it. Those who know the best and most certain way to get what they want deserve it the most. (*to the Duke of York*) Uncle, give me your hands. No, dry your eyes. Tears show love, but do nothing to fix their cause. (*to Henry Bolingbroke*) Cousin, I am too young to be your father, even though you are old enough to inherit my kingdom. I'll willingly give you what you want, because you've forced me to do it. So now you'll go to London, cousin?

HENRY BOLINGBROKE

> Yes, my good lord.

KING RICHARD II

> Then I can't say no.

Trumpets blow. They exit.

ACT 3, SCENE 4

Langley. The Duke of York's garden. Enter the QUEEN *and
two* LADIES

QUEEN

What sport shall we devise here in this garden,
To drive away the heavy thought of care?

LADY

Madam, we'll play at bowls.

QUEEN

'Twill make me think the world is full of rubs,
5   And that my fortune rubs against the bias.

LADY

Madam, we'll dance.

QUEEN

My legs can keep no measure in delight,
When my poor heart no measure keeps in grief.
Therefore, no dancing, girl; some other sport.

LADY

10   Madam, we'll tell tales.

QUEEN

Of sorrow or of joy?

LADY

Of either, madam.

QUEEN

Of neither, girl:
For of joy, being altogether wanting,
15   It doth remember me the more of sorrow;
Or if of grief, being altogether had,
It adds more sorrow to my want of joy.
For what I have I need not to repeat;
And what I want it boots not to complain.

LADY

20   Madam, I'll sing.

ACT 3, SCENE 4

*The village of Langley, in the Duke of York's garden.
The* QUEEN *enters, with two Ladies.*

QUEEN

What game should we play here in the garden to distract
us from our worries?

LADY

Madam, let's play **bowls**.

*A game played
by rolling slightly
asymmetrical
balls as close
as possible to
a white ball,
known as a jack.*

QUEEN

It will make me think the world is full of obstacles,
and that my fortune sends me the wrong way.

LADY

Madam, we'll dance.

QUEEN

My legs can't move with delight when my heart is so
full of grief. Therefore, no dancing, girl. Let's find some
other sport.

LADY

Madam, we'll tell stories.

QUEEN

Sad ones or happy ones?

LADY

Either, madam.

QUEEN

Neither, girl. Since I have no happiness, happy stories
only remind me of sorrow. Since I am full of grief, sad
stories only add more sorrow to my lack of happiness. I
don't need to add on to what I already have, and it does
no good to complain about what I want.

LADY

Madam, I'll sing.

QUEEN

                     'Tis well that thou hast cause
But thou shouldst please me better, wouldst thou weep.

LADY

I could weep, madam, would it do you good.

QUEEN

And I could sing, would weeping do me good,
25   And never borrow any tear of thee.

Enter a GARDENER, *and two* SERVANTS

But stay, here come the gardeners:
Let's step into the shadow of these trees.
My wretchedness unto a row of pins,
They'll talk of state; for every one doth so
30   Against a change; woe is forerun with woe.

                          QUEEN *and* LADIES *retire*

GARDENER

Go, bind thou up yon dangling apricocks,
Which, like unruly children, make their sire
Stoop with oppression of their prodigal weight.
Give some supportance to the bending twigs.
35   Go thou, and like an executioner,
Cut off the heads of too fast growing sprays,
That look too lofty in our commonwealth.
All must be even in our government.
You thus employ'd, I will go root away
40   The noisome weeds, which without profit suck
The soil's fertility from wholesome flowers.

SERVANT

Why should we in the compass of a pale
Keep law and form and due proportion,
Showing, as in a model, our firm estate,
45   When our sea-walled garden, the whole land,

QUEEN

It's wonderful that you are happy enough to sing, but it would make me happier if you wept.

LADY

If it would do you any good, madam, I could weep.

QUEEN

And if weeping would do me any good, I would do it enough that I'd be able to sing.

A GARDENER enters, with two Servants.

But stop, here come the gardeners. Let's move into the shadows of these trees. I'd only bet my most worthless possessions that they won't talk about politics, since that's what everyone does in anticipation of a change. Sorrow is always announced with sorrow.

The QUEEN and her Ladies step into the background.

GARDENER

Go, gather up those dangling apricots. The tree is bending under their excessive weight, like a father oppressed by his unruly children. Give the twigs some support. Cut off the branches that are growing too fast and high in our country. Everything must be equal. While you're doing that, I'll go dig up those harmful weeds that are stealing all the nutrients in the soil from the flowers.

SERVANT

Why should we make this garden look like a model of beauty and order when the whole country is in disarray? If England were a garden, it would be full of weeds, with the most beautiful flowers choked to death. All the fruit

Is full of weeds, her fairest flowers choked up,
Her fruit-trees all upturned, her hedges ruin'd,
Her knots disorder'd and her wholesome herbs
Swarming with caterpillars?

GARDENER

50   Hold thy peace:
He that hath suffer'd this disorder'd spring
Hath now himself met with the fall of leaf:
The weeds which his broad-spreading leaves did shelter,
That seem'd in eating him to hold him up,
55   Are pluck'd up root and all by Bolingbroke,
I mean the Earl of Wiltshire, Bushy, Green.

SERVANT

What, are they dead?

GARDENER

                              They are. And Bolingbroke
Hath seized the wasteful king. O, what pity is it
60   That he had not so trimm'd and dress'd his land
As we this garden! We at time of year
Do wound the bark, the skin of our fruit-trees,
Lest, being over-proud in sap and blood,
With too much riches it confound itself.
65   Had he done so to great and growing men,
They might have lived to bear and he to taste
Their fruits of duty. Superfluous branches
We lop away, that bearing boughs may live.
Had he done so, himself had borne the crown,
70   Which waste of idle hours hath quite thrown down.

SERVANT

What, think you then the king shall be deposed?

GARDENER

Depress'd he is already, and deposed
'Tis doubt he will be: letters came last night
To a dear friend of the good Duke of York's,
75   That tell black tidings.

trees would be torn out of the ground, the hedges would be ruined, the carefully designed flowerbeds would be a mess, and the herbs would be covered in caterpillars.

GARDENER

Be quiet. The one who allowed this disordered mess to grow is now withering like a tree in autumn. The weeds that he sheltered with his leaves, and that seemed to prop him up while simultaneously destroying him, have been ripped up by Bolingbroke. I'm talking about the Earl of Wiltshire, Bushy, and Green.

SERVANT

What, they are dead?

GARDENER

They are, and Bolingbroke has taken the wasteful king into custody. Oh, it's too bad that the king didn't take care of his land as carefully as we tend this garden! At this time of year we pierce the bark, so that the fruit trees aren't spoiled by too much of their own rich sap. If he had done the same thing to his men, who were spoiling from too much wealth and power, they might have served him better, and he would have profited. We cut the unnecessary branches off the trees, so that the ones that bear fruit will live. If he had done the same and cut away the unnecessary men in his service, he would still have the crown. But he wasted his time and lost it.

SERVANT

What, do you think the king will be dethroned?

GARDENER

He's already been brought low, and it's feared he'll be dethroned. A dear friend of the Duke of York received letters last night with bad news.

QUEEN

O, I am press'd to death through want of speaking!
                              (*Coming forward.*)
Thou, old Adam's likeness, set to dress this garden,
How dares thy harsh rude tongue sound this
        unpleasing news?
What Eve, what serpent, hath suggested thee
80   To make a second fall of cursed man?
Why dost thou say King Richard is deposed?
Darest thou, thou little better thing than earth,
Divine his downfall? Say, where, when, and how,
Camest thou by this ill tidings? speak, thou wretch.

GARDENER

85   Pardon me, madam. Little joy have I
To breathe this news; yet what I say is true.
King Richard, he is in the mighty hold
Of Bolingbroke. Their fortunes both are weigh'd.
In your lord's scale is nothing but himself,
90   And some few vanities that make him light;
But in the balance of great Bolingbroke,
Besides himself, are all the English peers,
And with that odds he weighs King Richard down.
Post you to London, and you will find it so.
95   I speak no more than everyone doth know.

QUEEN

Nimble mischance, that art so light of foot,
Doth not thy embassage belong to me,
And am I last that knows it? O, thou think'st
To serve me last, that I may longest keep
100   Thy sorrow in my breast. Come, ladies, go,
To meet at London London's king in woe.
What, was I born to this, that my sad look
Should grace the triumph of great Bolingbroke?
Gardener, for telling me these news of woe,
105   Pray God the plants thou graft'st may never grow.

Exeunt **QUEEN** *and* **LADIES**

NO FEAR SHAKESPEARE

QUEEN

> Oh, not saying anything is killing me!
>
> *(She comes forward.)*
>
> You, gardener, how dare you say such awful things?
> What snake has tempted you to invent a second fall of
> man? Why do you say that King Richard is deposed?
> Do you dare predict his downfall when you are as low as
> the dirt? Tell me where, when, and how you heard these
> terrible things. Speak, you wretch.

GARDENER

> Forgive me, madam. I'm not happy to say it, but it's true.
> Bolingbroke has captured King Richard. Their fortunes
> are being weighed out. Your lord has only himself and his
> vanity, which makes him lighter. Great Bolingbroke has
> all the English peers with him, and that gives him greater
> weight than King Richard. If you hurry to London, you'll
> see. I'm only saying what everyone knows.

QUEEN

> Why am I the last to hear this bad news that concerns
> me? I'll feel the sorrow the longest and yet I'm the last
> to know. Come, ladies, let's go. We must go to London
> to see the king in his sorrow. Was this why I was born,
> to show my sad face while great Bolingbroke triumphs?
> Gardener, for telling me this awful news, I pray that your
> plants never grow.

> *The* **QUEEN** *and her Ladies exit.*

GARDENER

Poor queen! So that thy state might be no worse,
I would my skill were subject to thy curse.
Here did she fall a tear; here in this place
I'll set a bank of rue, sour herb of grace.
110 Rue, even for ruth, here shortly shall be seen,
In the remembrance of a weeping queen.

Exeunt

GARDENER

Poor queen! I wish her curse would strike my skill if it would help her. Her tear fell right here. I'll plant rue there, since it is a bitter and sad herb. If only out of pity, rue will soon grow here in remembrance of a weeping queen.

They exit

ACT FOUR
SCENE 1

Westminster Hall. Enter, as to the Parliament, HENRY
BOLINGBROKE, DUKE OF AUMERLE, NORTHUMBERLAND,
HENRY PERCY, LORD FITZWATER, DUKE OF SURREY, *the*
BISHOP OF CARLISLE, *the* ABBOT OF WESTMINSTER, *and*
another Lord, Herald, Officers, and BAGOT

HENRY BOLINGBROKE
> Call forth Bagot.
> Now, Bagot, freely speak thy mind;
> What thou dost know of noble Gloucester's death,
> Who wrought it with the king, and who perform'd
5> The bloody office of his timeless end.

BAGOT
> Then set before my face the Lord Aumerle.

HENRY BOLINGBROKE
> Cousin, stand forth, and look upon that man.

BAGOT
> My Lord Aumerle, I know your daring tongue
> Scorns to unsay what once it hath deliver'd.
10> In that dead time when Gloucester's death was plotted,
> I heard you say, "Is not my arm of length,
> That reacheth from the restful English court
> As far as Calais, to mine uncle's head?"
> Amongst much other talk, that very time,
15> I heard you say that you had rather refuse
> The offer of an hundred thousand crowns
> Than Bolingbroke's return to England,
> Adding withal how blest this land would be
> In this your cousin's death.

ACT FOUR
SCENE 1

Westminster Hall. HENRY BOLINGBROKE *enters, with the same ceremony as if he were entering Parliament.* DUKE OF AUMERLE, NORTHUMBERLAND, HENRY PERCY, LORD FITZWATER, DUKE OF SURREY, *the* BISHOP OF CARLISLE, *the* ABBOT OF WESTMINSTER, *and another lord enter as well, as do a herald, some officers, and* BAGOT.

HENRY BOLINGBROKE

Call forward Bagot. Now, Bagot, speak freely. What do you know about noble Gloucester's death? Who conspired with the king to do it, and who actually killed him?

BAGOT

Bring Lord Aumerle forward.

HENRY BOLINGBROKE

Cousin, stand in front and look at that man.

BAGOT

My Lord Aumerle, I know you're too brave to deny what you've already said. While Gloucester's death was being plotted, I heard you say, "Isn't my arm long enough to reach from the peaceful English court to Calais, to strike at my uncle's head?" At that same time, I heard you say, among other things, that you would rather refuse a hundred thousand crowns than have Bolingbroke return to England. And you added that the country would be blessed if Bolingbroke, your cousin, died.

DUKE OF AUMERLE

20   Princes and noble lords,
        What answer shall I make to this base man?
        Shall I so much dishonor my fair stars,
        On equal terms to give him chastisement?
        Either I must, or have mine honor soil'd
25   With the attainder of his slanderous lips.
        There is my gage, the manual seal of death,
        That marks thee out for hell. I say, thou liest,
        And will maintain what thou hast said is false
        In thy heart-blood, though being all too base
30   To stain the temper of my knightly sword.

HENRY BOLINGBROKE

        Bagot, forbear; thou shalt not take it up.

DUKE OF AUMERLE

        Excepting one, I would he were the best
        In all this presence that hath moved me so.

LORD FITZWATER

        If that thy valor stand on sympathy,
35   There is my gage, Aumerle, in gage to thine,
        By that fair sun which shows me where thou stand'st,
        I heard thee say, and vauntingly thou spakest it
        That thou wert cause of noble Gloucester's death.
        If thou deny'st it twenty times, thou liest;
40   And I will turn thy falsehood to thy heart,
        Where it was forged, with my rapier's point.

DUKE OF AUMERLE

        Thou darest not, coward, live to see that day.

LORD FITZWATER

        Now by my soul, I would it were this hour.

DUKE OF AUMERLE

        Fitzwater, thou art damn'd to hell for this.

HENRY PERCY

45   Aumerle, thou liest. His honor is as true
        In this appeal as thou art all unjust;
        And that thou art so, there I throw my gage.

DUKE OF AUMERLE

> Princes and noble lords, how should I respond to this lowly man? Should I dishonor my rank as a noble by chastising him on equal terms? I guess I must, or let him ruin my honor with this slanderous accusation. There is my glove, the symbol of your death. I say you lie, and I'll confirm in combat that what you said is a lie, though I won't stain my knightly sword with your common blood.

HENRY BOLINGBROKE

> Bagot, restrain yourself. You will not retaliate.

DUKE OF AUMERLE

> Except for Bolingbroke, I wish Bagot were the most noble person here to have angered me like this.

LORD FITZWATER

> If your courage depends on rank, there is my glove, Aumerle, to match your glove. I swear by the sun that shows me where you are that I heard you boast that you caused Gloucester's death. Even if you deny it twenty times, you lie, and I'll put that lie back in your heart, where it came from, with my sword.

DUKE OF AUMERLE

> Coward, you wouldn't dare do it.

LORD FITZWATER

> By my soul, I wish I could do it right now.

DUKE OF AUMERLE

> Fitzwater, you'll be damned to hell for this.

HENRY PERCY

> Aumerle, you lie. His accusation is as true as your denial is false. And I'll prove that you lie by throwing down my glove. Take it up, if you dare.

To prove it on thee to the extremest point
Of mortal breathing. Seize it, if thou darest.

DUKE OF AUMERLE

50 An if I do not, may my hands rot off
And never brandish more revengeful steel
Over the glittering helmet of my foe!

LORD

I task the earth to the like, forsworn Aumerle;
And spur thee on with full as many lies
55 As may be hollow'd in thy treacherous ear
From sun to sun. There is my honor's pawn;
Engage it to the trial, if thou darest.

DUKE OF AUMERLE

Who sets me else? By heaven, I'll throw at all!
I have a thousand spirits in one breast,
60 To answer twenty thousand such as you.

DUKE OF SURREY

My Lord Fitzwater, I do remember well
The very time Aumerle and you did talk.

LORD FITZWATER

'Tis very true. You were in presence then,
And you can witness with me this is true.

DUKE OF SURREY

65 As false, by heaven, as heaven itself is true.

LORD FITZWATER

Surrey, thou liest.

DUKE OF SURREY

                              Dishonorable boy!
That lie shall lie so heavy on my sword,
That it shall render vengeance and revenge
70 Till thou the lie-giver and that lie do lie
In earth as quiet as thy father's skull.
In proof whereof, there is my honor's pawn.
Engage it to the trial, if thou darest.

DUKE OF AUMERLE

If I don't, may my hands rot away and never again lift my sword over the helmet of my enemy!

LORD

I'll throw down my glove to you, too, lying Aumerle. And I'll accuse you of lying right in your ear, from sunrise to sunset. There's my pledge of honor. Pick it up, if you dare.

DUKE OF AUMERLE

Who else challenges me? By heaven, I'll throw my glove at you all. My breast holds a thousand spirits that can outmatch twenty thousand like you.

DUKE OF SURREY

My lord Fitzwater, I remember very well when you and Aumerle spoke.

LORD FITZWATER

That's true, you were there. And you can be my witness that this is true.

DUKE OF SURREY

It's as false as heaven is true.

LORD FITZWATER

Surrey, you lie.

DUKE OF SURREY

Dishonorable boy! Your lie will give such weight to my sword that it will attack you in revenge until you're lying in the grave as quiet as your dead father. As proof, there's my glove. Take it up, if you dare.

LORD FITZWATER

How fondly dost thou spur a forward horse!
75 If I dare eat, or drink, or breathe, or live,
I dare meet Surrey in a wilderness,
And spit upon him, whilst I say he lies,
And lies, and lies. There is my bond of faith
To tie thee to my strong correction.
80 As I intend to thrive in this new world,
Aumerle is guilty of my true appeal.
Besides, I heard the banish'd Norfolk say
That thou, Aumerle, didst send two of thy men
To execute the noble duke at Calais.

DUKE OF AUMERLE

85 Some honest Christian trust me with a gage
That Norfolk lies. Here do I throw down this,
If he may be repeal'd, to try his honor.

HENRY BOLINGBROKE

These differences shall all rest under gage
Till Norfolk be repeal'd. Repeal'd he shall be,
90 And, though mine enemy, restored again
To all his lands and signories. When he's return'd,
Against Aumerle we will enforce his trial.

BISHOP OF CARLISLE

That honorable day shall ne'er be seen.
Many a time hath banish'd Norfolk fought
95 For Jesu Christ in glorious Christian field,
Streaming the ensign of the Christian cross
Against black pagans, Turks, and Saracens:
And toil'd with works of war, retired himself
To Italy; and there at Venice gave
100 His body to that pleasant country's earth,
And his pure soul unto his captain Christ,
Under whose colors he had fought so long.

HENRY BOLINGBROKE

Why, bishop, is Norfolk dead?

LORD FITZWATER

You taunt me so foolishly! As easily as I dare to eat or
drink or breathe or live, I dare to meet Surrey in a wild
place and spit on him, all the while declaring that he lies.
There is my response, so that you can't run away from
it. I intend to do well in this new kingdom, and Aumerle
is guilty. Besides, I heard the banished Duke of Norfolk,
Thomas Mowbray, say that you, Aumerle, sent two of
your men to kill the noble duke at Calais.

DUKE OF AUMERLE

Someone lend me a glove so I can prove that Mowbray
lies. Here, I throw down this, so that I may test his honor
if he's ever brought back.

HENRY BOLINGBROKE

All these quarrels will be put on hold until Mowbray is
recalled from exile, as he will be. Even though he is my
enemy, he'll be given back his land and titles. And when
he comes back, we'll have his trial against Aumerle.

BISHOP OF CARLISLE

That day will never happen. Many times did Mowbray
fight for Jesus Christ in battle and raised the Christian
cross against the black pagans, Turks, and Saracens.
Exhausted by war, he retired to Italy. He gave his body to
its soil in Venice and gave his pure soul to Christ, under
whose banner he fought for so long.

HENRY BOLINGBROKE

Why, bishop, is Mowbray dead?

BISHOP OF CARLISLE

As surely as I live, my lord.

HENRY BOLINGBROKE

105   Sweet peace conduct his sweet soul to the bosom
Of good old Abraham! Lords appellants,
Your differences shall all rest under gage
Till we assign you to your days of trial.

Enter DUKE OF YORK, *attended*

DUKE OF YORK

Great Duke of Lancaster, I come to thee
110   From plume-pluck'd Richard, who with willing soul
Adopts thee heir, and his high scepter yields
To the possession of thy royal hand.
Ascend his throne, descending now from him;
And long live Henry, fourth of that name!

HENRY BOLINGBROKE

115   In God's name, I'll ascend the regal throne.

BISHOP OF CARLISLE

Marry, God forbid!
Worst in this royal presence may I speak,
Yet best beseeming me to speak the truth.
Would God that any in this noble presence
120   Were enough noble to be upright judge
Of noble Richard! Then true noblesse would
Learn him forbearance from so foul a wrong.
What subject can give sentence on his king?
And who sits here that is not Richard's subject?
125   Thieves are not judged but they are by to hear,
Although apparent guilt be seen in them;
And shall the figure of God's majesty,
His captain, steward, deputy elect,
Anointed, crowned, planted many years,
130   Be judged by subject and inferior breath,
And he himself not present? O, forfend it, God,

BISHOP OF CARLISLE

As surely as I am alive, my lord.

HENRY BOLINGBROKE

May peace take his sweet soul to Abraham! Lords, we'll keep all these challenges until we can set days for your trials.

The DUKE OF YORK enters, with his attendants.

DUKE OF YORK

Great Duke of Lancaster, I come to you from humbled Richard, who is willing to make you his heir and yields his royal scepter to your hands. Take his throne from him, and long live Henry, the fourth king with that name!

HENRY BOLINGBROKE

In God's name, I'll take the royal throne.

BISHOP OF CARLISLE

God forbid! I'm the least worthy to speak in this noble company, but it's fitting that I, a clergyman, speak the truth. If only one of the nobles here were noble enough to judge Richard! Then he would restrain himself from committing such a wrong. What subject can pass judgment on his king? And who here isn't Richard's subject? Even thieves aren't judged unless they're present, even when they're obviously guilty. Shall the image of God's majesty, who is His chosen deputy and caretaker and has been so for many years, be judged by his inferiors without even being present? Oh, God, don't allow such refined souls in a Christian land to be so obscene. I'm speaking to subjects as a subject, because I've been moved by God to speak boldly for his king. You might call my Lord of Hereford here king, but

That in a Christian climate souls refined
Should show so heinous, black, obscene a deed!
I speak to subjects, and a subject speaks,
135   Stirr'd up by God, thus boldly for his king.
My Lord of Hereford here, whom you call king,
Is a foul traitor to proud Hereford's king:
And if you crown him, let me prophesy:
The blood of English shall manure the ground,
140   And future ages groan for this foul act;
Peace shall go sleep with Turks and infidels,
And in this seat of peace tumultuous wars
Shall kin with kin and kind with kind confound.
Disorder, horror, fear, and mutiny
145   Shall here inhabit, and this land be call'd
The field of Golgotha and dead men's skulls.
O, if you raise this house against this house,
It will the woefullest division prove
That ever fell upon this cursed earth.
150   Prevent it, resist it, let it not be so,
Lest child, child's children, cry against you woe!

NORTHUMBERLAND

Well have you argued, sir, and for your pains
Of capital treason we arrest you here.
My Lord of Westminster, be it your charge
155   To keep him safely till his day of trial.
May it please you, lords, to grant the commons' suit.

HENRY BOLINGBROKE

Fetch hither Richard, that in common view
He may surrender. So we shall proceed
Without suspicion.

DUKE OF YORK

160   I will be his conduct.

Exit

he is a traitor to his king. If you give him the crown,
I predict that the blood of the English will soak the
soil, and future generations will regret this act. Peace
will leave England and go to the Turks and infidels,
while we will have terrible wars that will pit families
against each other. Disorder, fear, mutiny, and
horror will live here, and it will be known as a place
of terror and skulls. If you **pit your family against
his**, it will prove to be the worst division ever to take
place on earth. Prevent it from happening. Don't let
it be so, or your children and your grandchildren will
lament your actions!

> That is, Lancaster against York.

NORTHUMBERLAND
You've argued well, and in return we're arresting
you for capital treason. My Lord of Westminster, it's
your responsibility to keep him safe until he goes on
trial. My lords, please grant the **commons' suit**.

HENRY OF BOLINGBROKE
Bring Richard here, so that he can surrender in
public. That way I can proceed without suspicion.

> The request of
> the House of
> Commons that
> Richard might
> have judgment
> decreed against
> him so that the
> causes of his
> disposition might
> be published
> and known to
> the people.

DUKE OF YORK
I'll escort him.

He exits.

HENRY BOLINGBROKE

> Lords, you that here are under our arrest,
> Procure your sureties for your days of answer.
> Little are we beholding to your love,
> And little look'd for at your helping hands.

Re-enter DUKE OF YORK, *with* KING RICHARD II, *and Officers bearing the regalia*

KING RICHARD II

165
> Alack, why am I sent for to a king,
> Before I have shook off the regal thoughts
> Wherewith I reign'd? I hardly yet have learn'd
> To insinuate, flatter, bow, and bend my limbs.
> Give sorrow leave awhile to tutor me

170
> To this submission. Yet I well remember
> The favors of these men. Were they not mine?
> Did they not sometime cry "All hail!" to me?
> So Judas did to Christ. But he, in twelve,
> Found truth in all but one; I, in twelve thousand, none.

175
> God save the king! Will no man say "amen?"
> Am I both priest and clerk? Well then, amen.
> God save the king! Although I be not he;
> And yet, amen, if heaven do think him me.
> To do what service am I sent for hither?

DUKE OF YORK

180
> To do that office of thine own good will
> Which tired majesty did make thee offer,
> The resignation of thy state and crown
> To Henry Bolingbroke.

KING RICHARD II

> Give me the crown. Here, cousin, seize the crown;

185
> Here cousin:
> On this side my hand, and on that side yours.
> Now is this golden crown like a deep well

HENRY BOLINGBROKE

You lords who are here under arrest, arrange for someone to pledge that you'll be here for your trial. I don't owe you anything, and I don't expect to receive any loyalty from you.

The DUKE OF YORK *enters with* KING RICHARD II. *Officers follow them holding the crown and the scepter, the symbols of the kingship.*

KING RICHARD II

Alas, why does the king call for me when I've only just resigned myself to give up the throne? I've hardly had time to learn to act like a subject, who has to indulge the king and bow to him. Give me some time with my sorrow so that I can learn how to submit to another. I still remember how these men used to serve me. Didn't they once cry out, "All hail!" to me? But then so did Judas to Christ once. But Christ had eleven honest followers out of twelve. I don't have one out of twelve thousand. God save the king! Won't anyone say amen? Do I have to both give the blessing and affirm it? Well then, amen. God save the king! Even though I am not the king. And yet, I'll say amen in case heaven still considers me the king. Why have you sent for me?

DUKE OF YORK

You have to give up your country and your crown to Henry Bolingbroke of your own free will, even though you've already given it over through your defeat.

KING RICHARD II

Give me the crown. Here, cousin, take the crown. Here cousin. I'll put my hand on this side of it, and you put yours on the other. Now this golden crown looks like a well that has two buckets, and raising one causes the

That owes two buckets, filling one another,
The emptier ever dancing in the air,
190   The other down, unseen and full of water:
That bucket down and full of tears am I,
Drinking my griefs, whilst you mount up on high.

HENRY BOLINGBROKE

I thought you had been willing to resign.

KING RICHARD II

My crown I am, but still my griefs are mine.
195   You may my glories and my state depose,
But not my griefs; still am I king of those.

HENRY BOLINGBROKE

Part of your cares you give me with your crown.

KING RICHARD II

Your cares set up do not pluck my cares down.
My care is loss of care, by old care done;
200   Your care is gain of care, by new care won.
The cares I give I have, though given away;
They tend the crown, yet still with me they stay.

HENRY BOLINGBROKE

Are you contented to resign the crown?

KING RICHARD II

Ay, no; no, ay; for I must nothing be;
205   Therefore no no, for I resign to thee.
Now mark me, how I will undo myself.
I give this heavy weight from off my head
And this unwieldy scepter from my hand,
The pride of kingly sway from out my heart.
210   With mine own tears I wash away my balm,
With mine own hands I give away my crown,
With mine own tongue deny my sacred state,
With mine own breath release all duty's rites.
All pomp and majesty I do forswear;
215   My manors, rents, revenues I forego;
My acts, decrees, and statutes I deny.

other to drop and fill up. One is empty and dances up in the air, while the other is down in the well and full of water. I'm the bucket at the bottom, full of tears, and you are the one risen to the top.

HENRY BOLINGBROKE

I thought you were willing to give up the crown.

KING RICHARD II

I'm willing to give up my crown, but my sadness is still mine. You can take my glory and my royal status, but I still rule over my grief.

HENRY BOLINGBROKE

You'll lose some of those worries when you give the crown to me.

KING RICHARD II

Just because you gain those worries doesn't mean I lose them. I'm worried by their loss and by what has happened. Your concern is the new responsibilities you are taking on. I'll keep my worries even if I give away their cause, the crown.

HENRY BOLINGBROKE

Are you willing to give up the crown?

KING RICHARD II

Yes and no. No and yes, since I must not be anything. So, no, no, because I give it up to you. Now look, I'll make myself nothing. I'll give you this heavy crown from my head, and this scepter from my hand. I'll take the pride of being king out of my heart. My own tears will wash away the oil that made me king. My own hands will give away the crown. My own tongue will deny my sacred right to be king. My own breath will give up all oaths of allegiance made to me. I give up all the ritual and ceremony, all my homes, my income, and reject all the laws I enacted. May God pardon everyone who breaks his oath to me! May God keep them from breaking their oath to you! Let me grieve for nothing since I have nothing, and let you be

God pardon all oaths that are broke to me!
God keep all vows unbroke that swear to thee!
Make me, that nothing have, with nothing grieved,
220   And thou with all pleased, that hast all achieved!
Long mayst thou live in Richard's seat to sit,
And soon lie Richard in an earthly pit!
God save King Harry, unking'd Richard says,
And send him many years of sunshine days!
225   What more remains?

NORTHUMBERLAND

                              No more, but that you read
These accusations and these grievous crimes
Committed by your person and your followers
Against the state and profit of this land;
230   That, by confessing them, the souls of men
May deem that you are worthily deposed.

KING RICHARD II

Must I do so? And must I ravel out
My weaved-up folly? Gentle Northumberland,
If thy offences were upon record,
235   Would it not shame thee in so fair a troop
To read a lecture of them? If thou wouldst,
There shouldst thou find one heinous article
Containing the deposing of a king
And cracking the strong warrant of an oath,
240   Mark'd with a blot, damn'd in the book of heaven—
Nay, all of you that stand and look upon me
Whilst that my wretchedness doth bait myself,
Though some of you with Pilate wash your hands
Showing an outward pity, yet you Pilates
245   Have here deliver'd me to my sour cross,
And water cannot wash away your sin.

NORTHUMBERLAND

My lord, dispatch; read o'er these articles.

pleased with everything since you have everything! May you live long in my place, and let me be buried soon! God save King Harry, former King Richard says, and let him have many happy days! What else is left?

NORTHUMBERLAND

Nothing but for you to read aloud all the accusations and crimes that you and your followers committed against the well-being and prosperity of this country. Once you've confessed, everyone can agree that you've been justly dethroned.

KING RICHARD II

Do I have to? Do I have to list out these charges? Dear Northumberland, if all your crimes were listed out, wouldn't you be ashamed to read them in front of such a distinguished group? If you did, you'd find on the list the terrible crime of deposing a king and breaking an oath, crimes condemned by heaven. All of you who are watching me act out my miserable fate here pretend like **Pilate** that you've done nothing wrong and look at me with pity. But you've all played a part in bringing me to this state, and you can't deny your sin.

The Roman governor of Judea who ordered the crucifixion of Jesus. He washed his hands to signify that the execution took place at the request of the Jews and he took no responsibility.

NORTHUMBERLAND

My lord, get on with it. Read the charges.

KING RICHARD II
Mine eyes are full of tears, I cannot see.
And yet salt water blinds them not so much
250   But they can see a sort of traitors here.
Nay, if I turn mine eyes upon myself,
I find myself a traitor with the rest;
For I have given here my soul's consent
To undeck the pompous body of a king,
255   Made glory base and sovereignty a slave,
Proud majesty a subject, state a peasant.

NORTHUMBERLAND
My lord—

KING RICHARD II
No lord of thine, thou haught insulting man,
Nor no man's lord. I have no name, no title,
260   No, not that name was given me at the font,
But 'tis usurp'd. Alack the heavy day,
That I have worn so many winters out
And know not now what name to call myself!
O that I were a mockery king of snow,
265   Standing before the sun of Bolingbroke,
To melt myself away in water drops!
Good king, great king, and yet not greatly good,
An if my word be sterling yet in England,
Let it command a mirror hither straight,
270   That it may show me what a face I have,
Since it is bankrupt of his majesty.

HENRY BOLINGBROKE
Go some of you and fetch a looking-glass.

Exit an attendant

NORTHUMBERLAND
Read o'er this paper while the glass doth come.

KING RICHARD II
Fiend, thou torment'st me ere I come to hell!

KING RICHARD II

My eyes are full of tears and I can't see. But even
so, I can see a group of traitors in front of me. And
if I look at myself, I see just as great a traitor. I've
agreed to give up my royal garments, made nobility
common, and made a master a slave. I've made a
king a subject and made the richest the poorest.

NORTHUMBERLAND

My lord—

KING RICHARD II

I'm not your lord, you haughty, insulting man. I'm no
man's lord. I don't have a name or a title. The name I
was baptized with is no longer mine. How sad it is that
I am so old and I don't know what to call myself! If only
I were a snowman, I could stand in front of the sun of
Bolingbroke and let myself be melted! Good king, great
king, but not a very good man. If my commands still have
value in England, let me command someone to bring me
a mirror, so I may see what I look like without any of my
noble majesty.

HENRY BOLINGBROKE

Someone go and get a mirror.

An attendant exits.

NORTHUMBERLAND

Read this paper until the mirror arrives.

KING RICHARD II

Fiend, you are torturing me before I even get to hell!

HENRY BOLINGBROKE

275   Urge it no more, my Lord Northumberland.

NORTHUMBERLAND

The commons will not then be satisfied.

KING RICHARD II

They shall be satisfied. I'll read enough,
When I do see the very book indeed
Where all my sins are writ, and that's myself.

Re-enter Attendant, with a glass

280   Give me the glass, and therein will I read.
No deeper wrinkles yet? Hath sorrow struck
So many blows upon this face of mine,
And made no deeper wounds? O flatt'ring glass,
Like to my followers in prosperity,
285   Thou dost beguile me! Was this face the face
That every day under his household roof
Did keep ten thousand men? Was this the face
That, like the sun, did make beholders wink?
Was this the face that faced so many follies,
290   And was at last outfaced by Bolingbroke?
A brittle glory shineth in this face:
As brittle as the glory is the face;

(He dashes the glass against the ground.)

For there it is, crack'd in a hundred shivers.
Mark, silent king, the moral of this sport,
295   How soon my sorrow hath destroy'd my face.

HENRY BOLINGBROKE

The shadow of your sorrow hath destroy'd
The shadow of your face.

KING RICHARD II

Say that again.
The shadow of my sorrow! Ha! Let's see:
300   'Tis very true, my grief lies all within;
And these external manners of laments

HENRY BOLINGBROKE

Lord Northumberland, stop asking him to read it.

NORTHUMBERLAND

The House of Commons won't be satisfied.

KING RICHARD II

They'll get what they want. I'll read it when I can look at my face and see the sins that appear there.

The ATTENDANT re-enters with a mirror.

Give me the mirror, and I'll read what's on my face. No deeper wrinkles yet? Could I endure so many sorrows without them appearing on my face? Oh flattering mirror, you are lying to me just like my followers did during happier times. Was this the same man who once kept ten thousand men in his employ? Was this the face that made men lower their gaze, as if they were looking into the sun? Was this the same face that endured so many challenges until it was defeated by Bolingbroke? There's a fragile glory in this face, and it's a face as fragile as glory.

(He throws the mirror on the ground.)

Look, there it is in a hundred pieces. Pay attention, king, to what this means. Sorrow has so quickly destroyed my face.

HENRY BOLINGBROKE

It's only the outward gloom of your sorrow that has destroyed the appearance of your face.

KING RICHARD II

Say that again. The outward gloom of my sorrow! Ha! Let's see. It's true that my grief is inside me and that anything I say or do to indicate my grief is just the outward reflection of what's inside. Thank you, king, for

Are merely shadows to the unseen grief
That swells with silence in the tortured soul.
There lies the substance: and I thank thee, king,
305   For thy great bounty, that not only givest
Me cause to wail but teachest me the way
How to lament the cause. I'll beg one boon,
And then be gone and trouble you no more.
Shall I obtain it?

HENRY BOLINGBROKE
310   Name it, fair cousin.

KING RICHARD II
"Fair cousin"? I am greater than a king:
For when I was a king, my flatterers
Were then but subjects. Being now a subject,
I have a king here to my flatterer.
315   Being so great, I have no need to beg.

HENRY BOLINGBROKE
Yet ask.

KING RICHARD II
And shall I have?

HENRY BOLINGBROKE
You shall.

KING RICHARD II
Then give me leave to go.

HENRY BOLINGBROKE
320   Whither?

KING RICHARD II
Whither you will, so I were from your sights.

HENRY BOLINGBROKE
Go, some of you convey him to the Tower.

KING RICHARD II
O, good! Convey? Conveyers are you all,
That rise thus nimbly by a true king's fall.

Exeunt **KING RICHARD II**, *some Lords, and a Guard*

being so kind as to not only give me reason to grieve but also to teach me how to show my grief. I'll beg one favor, and then I'll go away and no longer bother you. Will you give it to me?

HENRY BOLINGBROKE

Whatever you want, fair cousin.

KING RICHARD II

"Fair cousin"? I must be mightier than a king, since when I was a king subjects flattered me, but now that I'm a subject the king flatters me. Since I'm so mighty, I don't need to beg.

HENRY BOLINGBROKE

Ask anyway.

KING RICHARD II

And will I have it?

HENRY BOLINGBROKE

You will.

KING RICHARD II

Then give me permission to go.

HENRY BOLINGBROKE

Where?

KING RICHARD II

Wherever you want, as long as it is away from you.

HENRY BOLINGBROKE

Go, some of you take him to the tower.

KING RICHARD II

Oh good! Take me? You're all takers who've risen so mightily by my downfall.

KING RICHARD II *exits, with some lords and a guard.*

HENRY BOLINGBROKE

325   On Wednesday next we solemnly set down
Our coronation. Lords, prepare yourselves.

Exeunt all except the BISHOP OF CARLISLE, *the
Abbot of Westminster, and* DUKE OF AUMERLE

ABBOT

A woeful pageant have we here beheld.

BISHOP OF CARLISLE

The woe's to come. The children yet unborn.
Shall feel this day as sharp to them as thorn.

DUKE OF AUMERLE

330   You holy clergymen, is there no plot
To rid the realm of this pernicious blot?

ABBOT

My lord,
Before I freely speak my mind herein,
You shall not only take the sacrament
335   To bury mine intents, but also to effect
Whatever I shall happen to devise.
I see your brows are full of discontent,
Your hearts of sorrow and your eyes of tears.
Come home with me to supper. I'll lay
340   A plot shall show us all a merry day.

Exeunt

HENRY BOLINGBROKE

> Next Wednesday, I'll be crowned. Lords, prepare for it.

> *They all exit, except the* BISHOP OF CARLISLE, *the* ABBOT
> OF WESTMINSTER, *and the* DUKE OF AUMERLE.

ABBOT

> This is a sad scene we've witnessed.

BISHOP OF CARLISLE

> The sadness is yet to come. Children who aren't even
> born yet will feel the effects of this day like a thorn in
> their side.

DUKE OF AUMERLE

> You holy men, isn't there a way we can get rid of this
> terrible ruler?

ABBOT

> My lord, before I speak freely, you must swear to keep
> this a secret and also to promise that whatever plan I
> come up with is carried out. I see how unhappy you are.
> Come home with me for supper. I'll put forward a plot
> that will make us all happy.

> *They exit.*

ACT FIVE
SCENE 1

London. A street leading to the Tower. Enter QUEEN *and Ladies.*

QUEEN

    This way the king will come. This is the way
    To Julius Caesar's ill-erected tower,
    To whose flint bosom my condemned lord
    Is doom'd a prisoner by proud Bolingbroke.
5   Here let us rest, if this rebellious earth
    Have any resting for her true king's queen.

Enter KING RICHARD II *and Guard*

    But soft, but see, or rather do not see,
    My fair rose wither: yet look up, behold,
    That you in pity may dissolve to dew
10   And wash him fresh again with true-love tears.
    Ah, thou, the model where old Troy did stand,
    Thou map of honor, thou King Richard's tomb,
    And not King Richard! Thou most beauteous inn,
    Why should hard-favor'd grief be lodged in thee
15   When triumph is become an alehouse guest?

KING RICHARD II

    Join not with grief, fair woman, do not so,
    To make my end too sudden. Learn, good soul,
    To think our former state a happy dream;
    From which awaked, the truth of what we are
20   Shows us but this: I am sworn brother, sweet,
    To grim Necessity, and he and I
    Will keep a league till death. Hie thee to France
    And cloister thee in some religious house.
    Our holy lives must win a new world's crown,
25   Which our profane hours here have stricken down.

ACT FIVE
SCENE 1

London. A street leading to the Tower of London. The QUEEN *and ladies enter.*

QUEEN

The king will come this way as he is taken to the tower, where proud Bolingbroke condemned him to be held a prisoner. Let's rest here, if there is anywhere on this rebellious earth where I can rest.

KING RICHARD II *and guards enter.*

But wait, but look, or rather don't look or you will wither. No, but look up, and let pity wash over you and your tears of love bathe him. Ah, you, fallen in greatness like **Troy**, the epitome of honor. You look like a shell of King Richard and not King Richard himself. Oh, why should grief live in you, who are so honorable and royal, while triumph lives within Bolingbroke, a commoner?

The city besieged and destroyed by the Greeks in the Trojan War.

KING RICHARD II

Fair lady, don't grieve as if I were already dead. Think of our past as a happy dream and that we have simply awoken to reality. I've had to bow to necessity, and I'll stay that way until I die. Go quickly to France and join a convent. Our only hope is to become holy and be crowned in heaven, since our lives here have ended in such ruin.

QUEEN

    What, is my Richard both in shape and mind
    Transform'd and weaken'd? Hath Bolingbroke deposed
    Thine intellect? Hath he been in thy heart?
    The lion dying thrusteth forth his paw,
30   And wounds the earth, if nothing else, with rage
    To be o'erpower'd; and wilt thou, pupil-like,
    Take thy correction mildly, kiss the rod,
    And fawn on rage with base humility,
    Which art a lion and a king of beasts?

KING RICHARD II

35   A king of beasts, indeed. If aught but beasts,
    I had been still a happy king of men.
    Good sometime queen, prepare thee hence for France.
    Think I am dead and that even here thou takest,
    As from my deathbed, thy last living leave.
40   In winter's tedious nights sit by the fire
    With good old folks and let them tell thee tales
    Of woeful ages long ago betid;
    And ere thou bid good night, to quit their griefs,
    Tell thou the lamentable tale of me
45   And send the hearers weeping to their beds.
    For why, the senseless brands will sympathize
    The heavy accent of thy moving tongue
    And in compassion weep the fire out;
    And some will mourn in ashes, some coal-black,
50   For the deposing of a rightful king.

Enter NORTHUMBERLAND *and others*

NORTHUMBERLAND

    My lord, the mind of Bolingbroke is changed.
    You must to Pomfret, not unto the Tower.
    And, madam, there is order ta'en for you.
    With all swift speed you must away to France.

QUEEN

> What, has my Richard been changed and weakened in
> both body and mind? Has Bolingbroke overthrown your
> mind? Has he turned your heart? The dying lion claws
> at the earth, if nothing else, in his rage at being defeated.
> Will you act like a rebuked student and take your
> punishment meekly, kiss the cane that beats you, and
> return rage with humility, when you are a lion and king of
> beasts?

KING RICHARD II

> A king of beasts, indeed. If only they weren't beasts, I
> would still be a happy king of men. Good former queen,
> get ready to go to France. Think of me as dead, and
> say good-bye to me now as if I were on my deathbed.
> Through long winter nights sit by the fire with good
> people and let them tell you stories of sad times long ago.
> And before you say good night, tell them my sadder story
> and send them weeping to their beds. Even the firewood
> will sympathize and cry out their fires. And some will
> be so unhappy at the story of the overthrow of a rightful
> king that they will cover themselves in ashes.

NORTHUMBERLAND *and others enter.*

NORTHUMBERLAND

> My lord, Bolingbroke has changed his mind. You
> must go to **Pomfret** instead of the tower. And
> madam, he's made arrangements for you to go to
> France as quickly as possible.

*A castle in
Yorkshire.*

KING RICHARD II

55 Northumberland, thou ladder wherewithal
The mounting Bolingbroke ascends my throne,
The time shall not be many hours of age
More than it is ere foul sin gathering head
Shalt break into corruption. Thou shalt think,
60 Though he divide the realm and give thee half,
It is too little, helping him to all.
And he shall think that thou, which know'st the way
To plant unrightful kings, wilt know again,
Being ne'er so little urged, another way
65 To pluck him headlong from the usurped throne.
The love of wicked men converts to fear;
That fear to hate, and hate turns one or both
To worthy danger and deserved death.

NORTHUMBERLAND

My guilt be on my head, and there an end.
70 Take leave and part; for you must part forthwith.

KING RICHARD II

Doubly divorced! Bad men, you violate
A twofold marriage, 'twixt my crown and me,
And then betwixt me and my married wife.
Let me unkiss the oath 'twixt thee and me;
75 And yet not so, for with a kiss 'twas made.
Part us, Northumberland; I toward the north,
Where shivering cold and sickness pines the clime;
My wife to France, from whence, set forth in pomp,
She came adorned hither like sweet May,
80 Sent back like Hallowmas or short'st of day.

QUEEN

And must we be divided? Must we part?

KING RICHARD II

Ay, hand from hand, my love, and heart from heart.

QUEEN

Banish us both and send the king with me.

KING RICHARD II

Northumberland, Bolingbroke is mounting my throne on your ladder, but it won't take very long until you turn against each other. You'll think that even though he gives you half the kingdom, it's not enough, since you helped him get it all. And he'll think that you, who knows how to put undeserving kings in the throne, will know how to remove him from the stolen throne. Wicked men's love soon turns to fear, then to hate, and from there one or both of them will become dangerous and die a violent death.

NORTHUMBERLAND

My guilt is on my own head, and that's an end to it. Say good-bye and separate, for you must depart shortly.

An allusion to a passage in the book of Matthew in the Bible, in which the Jews were said to have stated at Jesus's trial: "His death be upon our heads, and the heads of our children."

KING RICHARD II

Twice divorced! You force me to divorce my crown and now my wife. I can't undo with a kiss the vows that bound us together, because they were sealed with a kiss. Separate us, Northumberland. I'll go to the north, where cold and sickness afflict the region. And my wife goes to France, from where she came with celebration like the spring, and now is sent back like the dead of winter.

QUEEN

And do we have to be separated?

KING RICHARD I

Yes, my love, our hands and our hearts must be divided.

QUEEN

Banish us both, and send the king with me.

NORTHUMBERLAND
    That were some love but little policy.

QUEEN
85   Then whither he goes, thither let me go.

KING RICHARD II
    So two, together weeping, make one woe.
    Weep thou for me in France, I for thee here;
    Better far off than near, be ne'er the near.
    Go, count thy way with sighs; I mine with groans.

QUEEN
90   So longest way shall have the longest moans.

KING RICHARD II
    Twice for one step I'll groan, the way being short,
    And piece the way out with a heavy heart.
    Come, come, in wooing sorrow let's be brief,
    Since, wedding it, there is such length in grief.
95   One kiss shall stop our mouths, and dumbly part;
    Thus give I mine, and thus take I thy heart.

QUEEN
    Give me mine own again. 'Twere no good part
    To take on me to keep and kill thy heart.
    So, now I have mine own again, be gone,
100   That I might strive to kill it with a groan.

KING RICHARD II
    We make woe wanton with this fond delay:
    Once more, adieu. The rest let sorrow say.

Exeunt

NORTHUMBERLAND

That might be an act of love, but it's not a smart policy.

QUEEN

Then wherever he goes, let me follow him.

KING RICHARD II

So the two of us together will make one big sorrow. Weep for me in France, and I'll weep for you here. It's better for us to be far away than near, and never near each other again. Go measure the distance in sighs, and I'll do the same with groans.

QUEEN

So the farther I go, the longer I will moan.

KING RICHARD II

Since my way is shorter, I'll groan twice for every step I take and make the way longer with a sad heart. Come, let's cut short this talk of grief, because we'll have long enough to live with it. Let's kiss once and quiet our mouths and part without any more words. I give you my heart and take yours with me.

QUEEN

Give me my heart back. It will only kill your heart if I take it. So now that I have my own heart back, go, so I can try to kill my own with mourning.

KING RICHARD II

We're only encouraging sorrow with this delay. Once more, good-bye. My grief will say the rest.

They exit.

ACT 5, SCENE 2

The Duke of York's palace. Enter DUKE OF YORK *and* DUCHESS
OF YORK

DUCHESS OF YORK
>My lord, you told me you would tell the rest,
>When weeping made you break the story off,
>of our two cousins coming into London.

DUKE OF YORK
>Where did I leave?

DUCHESS OF YORK

5
>   At that sad stop, my lord,
>Where rude misgovern'd hands from windows' tops
>Threw dust and rubbish on King Richard's head.

DUKE OF YORK
>Then, as I said, the duke, great Bolingbroke,
>Mounted upon a hot and fiery steed

10
>Which his aspiring rider seem'd to know,
>With slow but stately pace kept on his course,
>Whilst all tongues cried "God save thee, Bolingbroke!"
>You would have thought the very windows spake,
>So many greedy looks of young and old

15
>Through casements darted their desiring eyes
>Upon his visage, and that all the walls
>With painted imagery had said at once
>"Jesu preserve thee! Welcome, Bolingbroke!"
>Whilst he, from the one side to the other turning,

20
>Bareheaded, lower than his proud steed's neck,
>Bespake them thus: "I thank you, countrymen."
>And thus still doing, thus he pass'd along.

DUCHESS OF YORK
>Alack, poor Richard! Where rode he the whilst?

DUKE OF YORK
>As in a theater the eyes of men,

25
>After a well-graced actor leaves the stage,

ACT 5, SCENE 2

The DUKE OF YORK*'s palace. The* DUKE OF YORK *and the*
DUCHESS OF YORK *enter.*

DUCHESS OF YORK

My lord, you told me you would tell the rest of the story
about our two relatives coming to London, until weeping
made you stop.

DUKE OF YORK

Where did I stop the story?

DUCHESS OF YORK

At the sad place, my lord, when rude hands were
throwing dust and rubbish on King Richard's head from
the upper windows.

DUKE OF YORK

Then, as I said, the duke, great Bolingbroke, got on a
magnificent horse that seemed to know it was him and
kept going in a slow and stately way. All around, people
were calling, "God save you, Bolingbroke!" You would
have thought the windows themselves were talking.
Both old and young people were looking out on him with
happy desire, and on the painted walls all around was
written, "Jesus protect you! Welcome, Bolingbroke!"
Meanwhile, he was turning his head, bare of any helmet
and not even as tall as his horse's neck, and said, "I thank
you, countrymen." And he continued along saying this as
he went.

DUCHESS OF YORK

Alas, poor Richard? Where was he riding then?

DUKE OF YORK

People looked at him with the dissatisfaction they might
have for a supporting actor who comes on stage after

Are idly bent on him that enters next,
Thinking his prattle to be tedious;
Even so, or with much more contempt, men's eyes
Did scowl on gentle Richard. No man cried "God save him!"
30   No joyful tongue gave him his welcome home,
But dust was thrown upon his sacred head,
Which with such gentle sorrow he shook off,
His face still combating with tears and smiles,
The badges of his grief and patience,
35   That had not God, for some strong purpose, steel'd
The hearts of men, they must perforce have melted
And barbarism itself have pitied him.
But heaven hath a hand in these events,
To whose high will we bound our calm contents.
40   To Bolingbroke are we sworn subjects now,
Whose state and honor I for aye allow.

DUCHESS OF YORK

Here comes my son Aumerle.

DUKE OF YORK

                                    Aumerle that was;
But that is lost for being Richard's friend,
45   And, madam, you must call him Rutland now:
I am in parliament pledge for his truth
And lasting fealty to the new-made king.

Enter DUKE OF AUMERLE

DUCHESS OF YORK

Welcome, my son. Who are the violets now
That strew the green lap of the new-come spring?

DUKE OF AUMERLE

50   Madam, I know not, nor I greatly care not.
God knows I had as lief be none as one.

DUKE OF YORK

Well, bear you well in this new spring of time,
Lest you be cropp'd before you come to prime.

the star has left. They stared at him with contempt, and
no one cried out, "God save him!" No one welcomed
him back. Instead, they threw dust on his sacred head.
He shook it off with gentle sorrow, while he both cried
and smiled as he wrestled with grief and patience.
For some reason God must have hardened everyone's
hearts, otherwise they would have melted so that even a
barbarian would have pitied him. But heaven has ordered
all this, and we must follow its will. We are Bolingbroke's
subjects now, and I must forever acknowledge his rule
and honor.

DUCHESS OF YORK

Here comes my son Aumerle.

DUKE OF YORK

He was Duke of Aumerle, but because he was
Richard's friend, he has lost his title. You must call
him **Rutland** now. I've sworn in Parliament that he
will honor and obey our new king.

*He retains the
title of Earl of
Rutland.*

The **DUKE OF AUMERLE** *enters.*

DUCHESS OF YORK

Welcome, my son. Who are the new favorites of the king?

DUKE OF AUMERLE

Madam, I don't know and I don't care. God knows I
prefer just as much not to be one.

DUKE OF YORK

Well, watch your step in this new regime, or you'll die
before your time. What's the news from Oxford? Are the
jousts and festivities happening?

What news from Oxford? Do these those jousts and
    triumphs hold?

DUKE OF AUMERLE

55   For aught I know, my lord, they do.

DUKE OF YORK

You will be there, I know.

DUKE OF AUMERLE

If God prevent not, I purpose so.

DUKE OF YORK

What seal is that that hangs without thy bosom?
Yea, look'st thou pale? Let me see the writing.

DUKE OF AUMERLE

60   My lord, 'tis nothing.

DUKE OF YORK

                    No matter, then, who see it.
I will be satisfied; let me see the writing.

DUKE OF AUMERLE

I do beseech your grace to pardon me.
It is a matter of small consequence,

65   Which for some reasons I would not have seen.

DUKE OF YORK

Which for some reasons, sir, I mean to see.
I fear, I fear—

DUCHESS OF YORK

              What should you fear?
'Tis nothing but some bond, that he is enter'd into

70   For gay apparel 'gainst the triumph day.

DUKE OF YORK

Bound to himself! What doth he with a bond
That he is bound to? Wife, thou art a fool.
Boy, let me see the writing.

DUKE OF AUMERLE

I do beseech you, pardon me. I may not show it.

DUKE OF YORK

75   I will be satisfied. Let me see it, I say.

               (He plucks it out of his bosom and reads it.)
Treason! Foul treason! Villain! Traitor! Slave!

DUKE OF AUMERLE

> For all I know they are.

DUKE OF YORK

> You will be there, I know.

DUKE OF AUMERLE

> I mean to, unless God prevents it.

DUKE OF YORK

> What is the note that I see in your shirt? You've just gone white. Let me see what it says.

DUKE OF AUMERLE

> My lord, it's nothing.

DUKE OF YORK

> Then it doesn't matter who sees it. I want to see it, and I will.

DUKE OF AUMERLE

> I beg you to forgive me. It's a small matter, but one that I don't want to share for certain reasons.

DUKE OF YORK

> I want to see it because of those reasons. I fear—

DUCHESS OF YORK

> What should you fear? It's just a bill for some festive clothing for the celebration.

DUKE OF YORK

> A bill that he's wearing so close to himself! Wife, you are a fool. Boy, let me see what it says.

DUKE OF AUMERLE

> I beg you, forgive me. I can't show you.

DUKE OF YORK.

> I will see it.

> > *(He grabs it and reads it.)*
>
> Treason! Foul treason! Villain! Traitor! Slave!

DUCHESS OF YORK
What is the matter, my lord?

DUKE OF YORK
Ho! Who is within there?

Enter a Servant

Saddle my horse.
80   God for his mercy, what treachery is here!

DUCHESS OF YORK
Why, what is it, my lord?

DUKE OF YORK
Give me my boots, I say. Saddle my horse.
Now, by mine honor, by my life, by my troth,
I will appeach the villain.

DUCHESS OF YORK
85   What is the matter?

DUKE OF YORK
Peace, foolish woman.

DUCHESS OF YORK
I will not peace. What is the matter, Aumerle?

DUKE OF AUMERLE
Good mother, be content. It is no more
Than my poor life must answer.

DUCHESS OF YORK
90   Thy life answer!

DUKE OF YORK
Bring me my boots! I will unto the king.

Re-enter Servant with boots

DUCHESS OF YORK
Strike him, Aumerle. Poor boy, thou art amazed.
Hence, villain! Never more come in my sight.

DUKE OF YORK
Give me my boots, I say.

DUCHESS OF YORK

What is the matter, my lord?

DUKE OF YORK

Hey, who is inside?

A servant enters.

Saddle my horse. God have mercy, what treachery is this!

DUCHESS OF YORK

Why, what is it, my lord?

DUKE OF YORK

Give me my boots and saddle my horse. Now, by my honor, my life, and my vow, I will accuse the villain.

DUCHESS OF YORK

What's the matter?

DUKE OF YORK

Be quiet, foolish woman.

DUCHESS OF YORK

I won't be quiet. What is the matter, Aumerle?

DUKE OF AUMERLE

Good mother, don't worry. It is something that I have to answer with my own life.

DUCHESS OF YORK

Answer with your life!

DUKE OF YORK

Bring me my boots. I must go to the king.

The servant enters, carrying boots.

DUCHESS OF YORK

Hit **him**, Aumerle! Poor boy, you are distraught. Go away, villain! Don't come back.

> She's instructing her son to hit the servant

DUKE OF YORK

Give me my boots, I say.

DUCHESS OF YORK

95   Why, York, what wilt thou do?
        Wilt thou not hide the trespass of thine own?
        Have we more sons? Or are we like to have?
        Is not my teeming date drunk up with time?
        And wilt thou pluck my fair son from mine age,
100   And rob me of a happy mother's name?
        Is he not like thee? Is he not thine own?

DUKE OF YORK

        Thou fond mad woman,
        Wilt thou conceal this dark conspiracy?
        A dozen of them here have ta'en the sacrament,
105   And interchangeably set down their hands,
        To kill the king at Oxford.

DUCHESS OF YORK

        He shall be none.
        We'll keep him here. Then what is that to him?

DUKE OF YORK

        Away, fond woman! Were he twenty times my son,
110   I would appeach him.

DUCHESS OF YORK

        Hadst thou groan'd for him
        As I have done, thou wouldst be more pitiful.
        But now I know thy mind. Thou dost suspect
        That I have been disloyal to thy bed,
115   And that he is a bastard, not thy son.
        Sweet York, sweet husband, be not of that mind.
        He is as like thee as a man may be,
        Not like to me or any of my kin,
        And yet I love him.

DUKE OF YORK

120   Make way, unruly woman!

Exit

DUCHESS OF YORK

Why, York, what are you going to do? Won't you hide the crime of your own child? Do we have any other sons? Are we likely to have more? Aren't I too old to have children? And are you going to take away my son in my old age, so I can no longer call myself a mother? Doesn't he look like you? Isn't he your son?

DUKE OF YORK

Foolish madwoman, will you try to cover up this terrible conspiracy? A dozen have sworn and signed here that they'll kill the king at Oxford.

DUCHESS OF YORK

He won't be one of them. We'll keep him here, and then what will this affair have to do with him?

DUKE OF YORK

Get away, foolish woman! Even if he were my son twenty times over, I would accuse him.

DUCHESS OF YORK

If you had gone through labor with him as I had, you would be more sorrowful. But now I know what you think. You think that I've cheated on you, and that he's a bastard and not your son. Sweet York, my sweet husband, don't think that way. He looks as much like you as anyone could. He doesn't look anything like me, or like anyone in my family, but I still love him.

DUKE OF YORK

Make way, you wild woman!

He exits.

DUCHESS OF YORK
>   After, Aumerle! Mount thee upon his horse;
>   Spur post, and get before him to the king,
>   And beg thy pardon ere he do accuse thee.
>   I'll not be long behind. Though I be old,
125   I doubt not but to ride as fast as York.
>   And never will I rise up from the ground
>   Till Bolingbroke have pardon'd thee. Away, be gone!

Exeunt

DUCHESS OF YORK

Go after him, Aumerle! Take his horse, get to the king before him, and beg forgiveness before he can even accuse you. I'll be right behind. Though I am old, I can ride as fast as York. I'll prostrate myself before the king until he has forgiven you. Go on!

They exit

ACT 5, SCENE 3

A royal palace. Enter HENRY BOLINGBROKE, HENRY PERCY, *and other Lords*

HENRY BOLINGBROKE

Can no man tell me of my unthrifty son?
'Tis full three months since I did see him last.
If any plague hang over us, 'tis he.
I would to God, my lords, he might be found.
5   Inquire at London, 'mongst the taverns there,
For there, they say, he daily doth frequent,
With unrestrained loose companions,
Even such, they say, as stand in narrow lanes,
And beat our watch, and rob our passengers;
10   Which he, young wanton and effeminate boy,
Takes on the point of honor to support
So dissolute a crew.

HENRY PERCY

My lord, some two days since I saw the prince,
And told him of those triumphs held at Oxford.

HENRY BOLINGBROKE

15   And what said the gallant?

HENRY PERCY

His answer was, he would unto the stews,
And from the common'st creature pluck a glove,
And wear it as a favor; and with that
He would unhorse the lustiest challenger.

HENRY BOLINGBROKE

20   As dissolute as desperate. Yet through both
I see some sparks of better hope, which elder years
May happily bring forth. But who comes here?

Enter DUKE OF AUMERLE

ACT 5, SCENE 3

A royal palace. HENRY BOLINGBROKE, HENRY PERCY, *and other lords enter.*

HENRY BOLINGBROKE

Can't anyone tell me about my irresponsible son? It's been three months since I last saw him. He's the only trouble in my life. I want him found. Ask in London, around the bars there. They say he goes to them every day with immoral friends, the kind of people who ambush passersby in the street and beat and rob the guards. My pleasure-seeking son thinks it's a badge of honor to support such an awful crowd.

HENRY PERCY

My lord, two days ago I saw the prince and told him about the celebration at Oxford.

HENRY BOLINGBROKE

And what did he say?

HENRY PERCY

He said that he would go to the whorehouse and get a glove from the most promiscuous whore there to wear as a favor. And then he would win in the jousts.

HENRY BOLINGBROKE

Even if he is immoral and reckless, I still see some hope that his better qualities will emerge as he gets older. But who is approaching?

The DUKE OF AUMERLE *enters.*

DUKE OF AUMERLE
Where is the king?

HENRY BOLINGBROKE
What means our cousin, that he stares and looks
    so wildly?

DUKE OF AUMERLE
25   God save your grace! I do beseech your majesty,
To have some conference with your grace alone.

HENRY BOLINGBROKE
Withdraw yourselves, and leave us here alone.

Exeunt HENRY PERCY *and Lords*

What is the matter with our cousin now?

DUKE OF AUMERLE
For ever may my knees grow to the earth,
30   My tongue cleave to my roof within my mouth
Unless a pardon ere I rise or speak.

HENRY BOLINGBROKE
Intended or committed was this fault?
If on the first, how heinous e'er it be,
To win thy after-love I pardon thee.

DUKE OF AUMERLE
35   Then give me leave that I may turn the key,
That no man enter till my tale be done.

HENRY BOLINGBROKE
Have thy desire.

DUKE OF YORK
(*within*) My liege, beware! Look to thyself!
Thou hast a traitor in thy presence there.

HENRY BOLINGBROKE
40   Villain, I'll make thee safe.

(Drawing.)

DUKE OF AUMERLE

> Where is the king?

HENRY BOLINGBROKE

> Why does my cousin stare and look about him so wildly?

DUKE OF AUMERLE

> God save your grace! I beg to speak to you alone.

HENRY BOLINGBROKE

> Go away, and leave us here alone.

> > **HENRY PERCY** *and lords exit.*

> What is the matter with you now?

DUKE OF AUMERLE

> May my knees remain on the ground and my tongue stay silent until you give me your forgiveness.

HENRY BOLINGBROKE

> Is it an offense that you have committed or that you planned to commit? If it was planned only, no matter how terrible it is, I'll forgive you in order to win your love.

DUKE OF AUMERLE

> Then let me lock the door so no one else can come in until I'm finished telling you.

HENRY BOLINGBROKE

> Go ahead.

DUKE OF YORK

> (*speaking from offstage*) My lord, beware. Watch yourself. You have a traitor with you.

HENRY BOLINGBROKE

> Villain, I'll render you harmless.

> > *(He draws his sword.)*

DUKE OF AUMERLE
>Stay thy revengeful hand; thou hast no cause to fear.

DUKE OF YORK
>(*within*) Open the door, secure, foolhardy king!
>Shall I for love speak treason to thy face?
>Open the door, or I will break it open.

Enter **DUKE OF YORK**

HENRY BOLINGBROKE
45
>What is the matter, uncle? Speak.
>Recover breath; tell us how near is danger,
>That we may arm us to encounter it.

DUKE OF YORK
>Peruse this writing here, and thou shalt know
>The treason that my haste forbids me show.

DUKE OF AUMERLE
50
>Remember, as thou read'st, thy promise pass'd.
>I do repent me. Read not my name there.
>My heart is not confederate with my hand.

DUKE OF YORK
>It was, villain, ere thy hand did set it down.
>I tore it from the traitor's bosom, king.
55
>Fear, and not love, begets his penitence.
>Forget to pity him, lest thy pity prove
>A serpent that will sting thee to the heart.

HENRY BOLINGBROKE
>O heinous, strong and bold conspiracy!
>O loyal father of a treacherous son!
60
>Thou sheer, immaculate, and silver fountain,
>From when this stream through muddy passages
>Hath held his current and defiled himself!
>Thy overflow of good converts to bad,
>And thy abundant goodness shall excuse
65
>This deadly blot in thy digressing son.

DUKE OF AUMERLE

> Hold off from your revenge. You don't have any reason to
> be afraid.

DUKE OF YORK

> (*speaking from offstage*) Open the door, my foolish king.
> Should I harshly criticize you out of love for you? Open
> the door, or I'll break it down.

The DUKE OF YORK *enters.*

HENRY BOLINGBROKE

> What is the matter, uncle? Tell me. Catch your breath.
> Tell me how close the danger is so that I can prepare for it.

DUKE OF YORK

> Read this, and you'll know what treason made me hurry
> so fast that I can hardly speak.

DUKE OF AUMERLE

> Remember, as you read, what you just promised.
> I already regret it. Don't read my name there. My heart
> doesn't match what my hand wrote.

DUKE OF YORK

> Villain, your heart believed it before your hand wrote it.
> I took the paper from the traitor, king. He regrets it out of
> fear, not out of love for you. Don't pity him, because that
> pity will come back to harm you.

HENRY BOLINGBROKE

> Oh, what a terrible and bold conspiracy! Oh, loyal father
> of a treacherous son! Your pure goodness overwhelms the
> wrongdoing of your foul son. Because you have proven
> yourself so loyal, I'll forgive your son's damnable crime.

DUKE OF YORK

So shall my virtue be his vice's bawd;
And he shall spend mine honor with his shame,
As thriftless sons their scraping fathers' gold.
Mine honor lives when his dishonor dies,
70   Or my shamed life in his dishonor lies.
Thou kill'st me in his life; giving him breath,
The traitor lives, the true man's put to death.

DUCHESS OF YORK

(*within*) What ho, my liege! For God's sake, let me in.

HENRY BOLINGBROKE

What shrill-voiced suppliant makes this eager cry?

DUCHESS OF YORK

75   A woman, and thy aunt, great king. 'Tis I.
Speak with me, pity me, open the door!
A beggar begs that never begg'd before.

HENRY BOLINGBROKE

Our scene is alter'd from a serious thing
And now changed to "The Beggar and the King."
80   My dangerous cousin, let your mother in.
I know she is come to pray for your foul sin.

DUKE OF YORK

If thou do pardon, whosoever pray,
More sins for this forgiveness prosper may.
This fester'd joint cut off, the rest rest sound;
85   This let alone will all the rest confound.

Enter DUCHESS OF YORK

DUCHESS OF YORK

O king, believe not this hard-hearted man!
Love loving not itself none other can.

DUKE OF YORK

Thou frantic woman, what dost thou make here?
Shall thy old dugs once more a traitor rear?

NO FEAR SHAKESPEARE

DUKE OF YORK

So my virtue will pay for his vice, and as some bad sons spend all their fathers' money, he'll spend all my honor with his shame. My honor can only live if his dishonor dies, otherwise I will live in shame. By forgiving him you are killing me. If he lives, so does a traitor, and the loyal man is put to death.

DUCHESS OF YORK

(*speaking from offstage*) Hello, my lord! For God's sake, let me in.

HENRY BOLINGBROKE

What screeching beggar is there?

DUCHESS OF YORK

A woman and your aunt, great king. It's me. Please pity me. Open the door and talk to me. I, who have never begged before, am now a beggar.

HENRY BOLINGBROKE

Suddenly the scene has changed from something serious to **"The Beggar and the King."** My dangerous cousin, let your mother in. I know that she's come to beg forgiveness for your terrible crime.

An old English ballad that was popular in Shakespeare's time.

DUKE OF YORK

No matter who prays, if you forgive this crime, only more will follow. By cutting off this infected limb you'll keep the rest of the body healthy. It's the only way to keep this sickness from spreading.

The DUCHESS OF YORK *enters.*

DUCHESS OF YORK

Oh, king, don't believe this hard-hearted man! If he can't love his son, he is incapable of loving anyone.

DUKE OF YORK

You crazy woman, what are you doing here? Are you going to nurse another traitor with your old breasts?

DUCHESS OF YORK

90   Sweet York, be patient. Hear me, gentle liege.

(She kneels.)

HENRY BOLINGBROKE

Rise up, good aunt.

DUCHESS OF YORK

Not yet, I thee beseech.
Forever will I walk upon my knees
And never see day that the happy sees,
95   Till thou give joy; until thou bid me joy,
By pardoning Rutland, my transgressing boy.

DUKE OF AUMERLE

Unto my mother's prayers I bend my knee.

DUKE OF YORK

Against them both my true joints bended be.
Ill mayst thou thrive, if thou grant any grace!

DUCHESS OF YORK

100   Pleads he in earnest? Look upon his face.
His eyes do drop no tears, his prayers are in jest;
His words come from his mouth, ours from our breast.
He prays but faintly and would be denied.
We pray with heart and soul and all beside.
105   His weary joints would gladly rise, I know.
Our knees shall kneel till to the ground they grow.
His prayers are full of false hypocrisy;
Ours of true zeal and deep integrity.
Our prayers do outpray his; then let them have
110   That mercy which true prayer ought to have.

HENRY BOLINGBROKE

Good aunt, stand up.

DUCHESS OF YORK

Nay, do not say "stand up."
Say "pardon" first and afterwards "stand up."
And if I were thy nurse, thy tongue to teach,
115   "Pardon" should be the first word of thy speech.
I never long'd to hear a word till now.

DUCHESS OF YORK

Sweet York, be patient. Gentle king, listen to me.

(She kneels.)

HENRY BOLINGBROKE

Get up, good aunt.

DUCHESS OF YORK

Not yet, I beg you. I'll stay on my knees and never look up again until you give me joy by forgiving Rutland, my wayward son.

DUKE OF AUMERLE

I'll kneel, too, in support of my mother's prayers.

DUKE OF YORK

I'll kneel to oppose them. If you forgive him, you'll only nurture more bad deeds.

DUCHESS OF YORK

Is he serious? Look at his face. He's not crying. His prayers are a joke. His words come from his mouth, but ours come from our hearts. He prays softly, hoping to be denied. We pray with heart and soul and all our bodies. I know his old and tired knees would like to straighten up. We'll stay kneeling till our knees grow roots in the ground. His prayers are hypocritical, while ours are full of true desire and integrity. Our prayers are more prayer-like than his, so let our prayers be rewarded as they ought to be, with mercy.

HENRY BOLINGBROKE

Good aunt, stand up.

DUCHESS OF YORK

No, don't say, "Stand up." First say, "I forgive," and then you can tell me to stand up. If I were your nanny, the first word I would teach you would be "pardon." I've never wanted to hear a word so badly. Say "pardon," king. Let pity teach you how. The word is short and sweeter than it

Say "pardon," king; let pity teach thee how.
The word is short, but not so short as sweet.
No word like "pardon" for kings' mouths so meet.

DUKE OF YORK

120   Speak it in French, king; say, "pardonne moi."

DUCHESS OF YORK

Dost thou teach pardon pardon to destroy?
Ah, my sour husband, my hard-hearted lord,
That set'st the word itself against the word!
Speak "pardon" as 'tis current in our land;
125   The chopping French we do not understand.
Thine eye begins to speak; set thy tongue there;
Or in thy piteous heart plant thou thine ear;
That hearing how our plaints and prayers do pierce,
Pity may move thee "pardon" to rehearse.

HENRY BOLINGBROKE

130   Good aunt, stand up.

DUCHESS OF YORK

                                    I do not sue to stand.
Pardon is all the suit I have in hand.

HENRY BOLINGBROKE

I pardon him, as God shall pardon me.

DUCHESS OF YORK

O happy vantage of a kneeling knee!
135   Yet am I sick for fear. Speak it again.
Twice saying "pardon" doth not pardon twain,
But makes one pardon strong.

HENRY BOLINGBROKE

I pardon him with all my heart

DUCHESS OF YORK

A god on Earth thou art.

HENRY BOLINGBROKE

140   But for our trusty brother-in-law and the abbot,
With all the rest of that consorted crew,
Destruction straight shall dog them at the heels.
Good uncle, help to order several powers

is short. It's the most fitting word for a king to say.

DUKE OF YORK

Say it in French, king. Say, *"Pardonne moi."*

French for
"Excuse me."

DUCHESS OF YORK

Do you try to destroy forgiveness by teaching that pardon? Oh, my sour husband, my hard-hearted lord, you'd make that word the opposite of what it means. Say "pardon" in English. We don't understand French. I can see it in your eyes, so let your tongue say it. Listen to the pity in your heart with your ears, which our laments and prayers pierce, so that pity may move you to say "pardon."

HENRY BOLINGBROKE

Good aunt, stand up.

DUCHESS OF YORK

I'm not begging to stand. All I want is a pardon.

HENRY OF BOLINGBROKE

I pardon him, as God will one day pardon me.

DUCHESS OF YORK

Oh, the happy view from a bended knee! But I'm still fearful. Say it again. Saying it twice doesn't divide your pardon and weaken it but makes the one pardon stronger.

HENRY BOLINGBROKE

With all my heart, I pardon him.

DUCHESS OF YORK

You are a god on earth.

HENRY BOLINGBROKE

But my trusted brother-in-law, the abbot, and all the rest of that group of conspirators must be destroyed. Good uncle, send several men to Oxford or wherever these traitors are hiding. I swear that as long as they are alive,

To Oxford, or where'er these traitors are.
145   They shall not live within this world, I swear,
But I will have them, if I once know where.
Uncle, farewell; and, cousin too, adieu.
Your mother well hath pray'd, and prove you true.

DUCHESS OF YORK

Come, my old son. I pray God make thee new.

Exeunt

I will find them and capture them. Uncle, good-bye, and good-bye cousin, too. Your mother has prayed well and proved your loyalty.

DUCHESS OF YORK
Come, my son. I'll pray that God forces you to reform.

They exit.

ACT 5, SCENE 4

The royal palace. Enter EXTON *and Servant.*

EXTON

Didst thou not mark the king, what words he spake,
"Have I no friend will rid me of this living fear?"
Was it not so?

SERVANT

These were his very words.

EXTON

5   "Have I no friend?" quoth he. He spake it twice,
And urged it twice together, did he not?

SERVANT

He did.

EXTON

And speaking it, he wistly look'd on me,
And who should say, "I would thou wert the man
10   That would divorce this terror from my heart"—
Meaning the king at Pomfret. Come, let's go.
I am the king's friend, and will rid his foe.

Exeunt

ACT 5, SCENE 4

The royal palace. EXTON *and a* SERVANT *enter.*

EXTON

> Didn't you notice the king and hear what he said? "Don't
> I have any friends who will rid me of this constant fear?"
> Didn't he say that?

SERVANT

> Those were his exact words.

EXTON

> Twice he said, "Don't I have any friends?" didn't he?

SERVANT

> He did.

EXTON

> And when he said it, he looked at me intently, as if he
> were saying, "I wish you were the man who would take
> this fear away from me." He means the king at Pomfret.
> Come, let's go. I am the king's friend, and I'll get rid him
> of his enemy.

They exit.

ACT 5, SCENE 5

Pomfret Castle. Enter KING RICHARD

KING RICHARD II

I have been studying how I may compare
This prison where I live unto the world:
And for because the world is populous
And here is not a creature but myself,
5   I cannot do it. Yet I'll hammer it out.
My brain I'll prove the female to my soul,
My soul the father, and these two beget
A generation of still-breeding thoughts,
And these same thoughts people this little world,
10   In humors like the people of this world,
For no thought is contented. The better sort,
As thoughts of things divine, are intermix'd
With scruples and do set the word itself
Against the word, as thus: "Come, little ones,"
15   And then again,
"It is as hard to come as for a camel
To thread the postern of a small needle's eye."
Thoughts tending to ambition, they do plot
Unlikely wonders; how these vain weak nails
20   May tear a passage through the flinty ribs
Of this hard world, my ragged prison walls,
And, for they cannot, die in their own pride.
Thoughts tending to content flatter themselves
That they are not the first of fortune's slaves,
25   Nor shall not be the last; like silly beggars
Who sitting in the stocks refuge their shame,
That many have and others must sit there;
And in this thought they find a kind of ease,
Bearing their own misfortunes on the back
30   Of such as have before endured the like.
Thus play I in one person many people,

ACT 5, SCENE 5

The castle at Pomfret. KING RICHARD *enters.*

KING RICHARD II

I have been thinking about how I might compare this
prison I live in to the world. But because the world
is full of people and I'm the only one here, I cannot
do it. Yet I'll work it out. My brain and my soul will
produce enough thoughts to fill this little world, like
people in the outside world and just as discontented.
The better kind of thought, like the thought of divine
things, is mixed with doubts and compares passages
from scripture, like **"Come, little ones"** and **"It is
as hard for a rich man to enter heaven as for a
camel to pass through a needle's eye."** Ambitious
thoughts plot unlikely miracles, such as digging
through the walls of my cell by hand, and these
thoughts die in their prime because they are futile.
Contented thoughts tell themselves that they aren't
the first to be a slave to fortune, and they won't be
the last. They're like beggars in the stocks who take
comfort in the fact that others have already sat there
and more will sit there. So I host many people inside
my own head, and none are content. Sometimes I'm
king, and then some treason makes me wish I was
a beggar, and so then I am a beggar. Then terrible
poverty persuades me that I was better off as king,
so then I am king again. And then I think that I have
been dethroned by Bolingbroke, and suddenly I'm
nothing. But whatever I am, just like all men, I'll
never be happy until I am dead and nothing at all.

> *Both passages
> involve the
> ease—or
> difficulty—of
> reaching heaven.*

And none contented. Sometimes am I king.
Then treasons make me wish myself a beggar,
And so I am. Then crushing penury
35   Persuades me I was better when a king.
Then am I king'd again, and by and by
Think that I am unking'd by Bolingbroke,
And straight am nothing. But whate'er I be,
Nor I nor any man that but man is
40   With nothing shall be pleased, till he be eased
With being nothing. Music do I hear?

(Music.)

Ha, ha! Keep time: how sour sweet music is,
When time is broke and no proportion kept!
So is it in the music of men's lives.
45   And here have I the daintiness of ear
To check time broke in a disorder'd string;
But for the concord of my state and time
Had not an ear to hear my true time broke.
I wasted time, and now doth time waste me;
50   For now hath time made me his numbering clock.
My thoughts are minutes; and with sighs they jar
Their watches on unto mine eyes, the outward watch,
Whereto my finger, like a dial's point,
Is pointing still, in cleansing them from tears.
55   Now sir, the sound that tells what hour it is
Are clamorous groans, which strike upon my heart,
Which is the bell. So sighs and tears and groans
Show minutes, times, and hours. But my time
Runs posting on in Bolingbroke's proud joy,
60   While I stand fooling here, his Jack o' the clock.
This music mads me. Let it sound no more,
For though it have holp madmen to their wits,
In me it seems it will make wise men mad.
Yet blessing on his heart that gives it me!
65   For 'tis a sign of love; and love to Richard
Is a strange brooch in this all-hating world.

Do I hear music?

(Music plays.)

Ha! Keep time. How awful music is when they don't keep time and the notes' proportions are ruined. It's the same thing in men's lives. And here I can chastise the poor time kept on an out-of-tune instrument, when in the harmony of my government and life I couldn't hear my own time breaking. I wasted time then, and now time wastes me. Time has made me his clock: my thoughts have become minutes that turn the clock hands in my eyes, and my finger is the dial that wipes away my tears. Now, sir, my groans are like the sounds that toll the hours, and they're made by striking my heart, which is the bell. Thus my sighs, tears, and groans signify minutes and hours. Meanwhile, my time speeds on as Bolingbroke has his joy, and I'm left here playing the clock for him. This music makes me crazy. Let it stop. It might make madmen sane, but for me, it makes a wise man mad. Yet bless the heart that plays it for me! It's a sign of love, and I am seldom given love in this hateful world.

Enter a GROOM *of the Stable*

GROOM

Hail, royal prince!

KING RICHARD II

Thanks, noble peer;

The cheapest of us is ten groats too dear.

70 What art thou? And how comest thou hither,

Where no man never comes but that sad dog

That brings me food to make misfortune live?

GROOM

I was a poor groom of thy stable, king,

When thou wert king; who, traveling towards York,

75 With much ado at length have gotten leave

To look upon my sometimes royal master's face.

O, how it yearn'd my heart when I beheld

In London streets, that coronation day,

When Bolingbroke rode on roan Barbary,

80 That horse that thou so often hast bestrid,

That horse that I so carefully have dress'd!

KING RICHARD II

Rode he on Barbary? Tell me, gentle friend,

How went he under him?

GROOM

So proudly as if he disdain'd the ground.

KING RICHARD II

85 So proud that Bolingbroke was on his back!

That jade hath eat bread from my royal hand;

This hand hath made him proud with clapping him.

Would he not stumble? Would he not fall down,

Since pride must have a fall, and break the neck

90 Of that proud man that did usurp his back?

Forgiveness, horse! Why do I rail on thee,

Since thou, created to be awed by man,

Wast born to bear? I was not made a horse;

And yet I bear a burthen like an ass,

95 Spurr'd, gall'd, and tired by jouncing Bolingbroke.

Enter a GROOM *of the stable.*

GROOM

Hello, royal prince!

KING RICHARD II

Thanks, my noble peer. You overvalue me, for we are equals and worth the same. Who are you, and how have you come here? My only visitor is that man who keeps my misfortune alive by bringing me food.

GROOM

I was a poor groom in your stable, king, when you were king. I was traveling toward York, and after a great deal of trouble I got permission to see my former master's face. Oh, how it saddened me when I saw Bolingbroke ride into London that coronation day on Barbary, the horse you've ridden so often and which I'd so often made ready for you!

KING RICHARD II

Did he ride on Barbary? Tell me, dear friend, how did the horse do?

GROOM

He pranced as proudly as if he scorned the earth.

KING RICHARD II

So proud to have Bolingbroke on his back! He had eaten bread from my hand, and I made him proud by patting his neck. Shouldn't he stumble? Shouldn't he fall down and break the neck of the man that stole my throne? I forgive you, horse! Why should I curse you, since you were created to fear man and carry him. I was not made like a horse, but I carry a burden like a donkey, and I'm kicked and exhausted from carrying rough-riding Bolingbroke.

Enter KEEPER, *with a dish*

KEEPER

Fellow, give place; here is no longer stay.

KING RICHARD II

If thou love me, 'tis time thou wert away.

GROOM

What my tongue dares not, that my heart shall say.

Exit

KEEPER

My lord, will't please you to fall to?

KING RICHARD II

100   Taste of it first, as thou art wont to do.

KEEPER

My lord, I dare not. Sir Pierce of Exton,
Who lately came from the king, commands the contrary.

KING RICHARD II

The devil take Henry of Lancaster and thee!
Patience is stale, and I am weary of it.

(He beats the keeper.)

KEEPER

105   Help, help, help!

Enter EXTON *and Servants, armed*

KING RICHARD II

How now! What means death in this rude assault?
Villain, thy own hand yields thy death's instrument.
        (Snatching an axe from a servant and killing him.)
Go thou, and fill another room in hell.
        (He kills another; then Exton strikes him down.)
That hand shall burn in never-quenching fire
110   That staggers thus my person. Exton, thy fierce hand
Hath with the king's blood stain'd the king's own land.
Mount, mount, my soul! Thy seat is up on high;
Whilst my gross flesh sinks downward, here to die.

Dies

The KEEPER *enters, with a dish.*

KEEPER

Fellow, go away. You can't stay any longer.

KING RICHARD II

If you love me, you should go.

GROOM

I don't dare say what my heart feels.

He exits.

KEEPER

My lord, will you eat?

KING RICHARD II

Taste it first, as you usually do.

KEEPER

My lord, I don't dare. Sir Pierce of Exton, who just arrived from the king, ordered me not to.

KING RICHARD II

May the devil take Henry of Lancaster and you! I am tired of being patient.

(He beats the keeper.)

KEEPER

Help, help, help!

EXTON *and servants enter, with weapons.*

KING RICHARD II

Do you mean to kill me in this despicable assault?
Villain, I'll kill you with your own weapon.
(He snatches an axe from a servant and kills him.)
Go to hell.
(He kills another, and then Exton strikes him down.)
You'll burn in hell forever for killing me. Exton, you've stained the king's land with the king's own blood. Arise my soul! Your place is in heaven, while my body sinks down and dies.

He dies.

EXTON

     As full of valor as of royal blood.
115   Both have I spill'd. O, would the deed were good!
     For now the devil, that told me I did well,
     Says that this deed is chronicled in hell.
     This dead king to the living king I'll bear
     Take hence the rest, and give them burial here.

Exeunt

EXTON

> He is as full of courage as of royal blood, which I've spilled here. I wish the deed were good! The devil, who told me that I did well, tells me now that I'll go to hell. I'll take this dead king to the living king and bury the others here.

They exit.

ACT 5, SCENE 6

Windsor Castle. Flourish. Enter HENRY BOLINGBROKE, DUKE
OF YORK, *with other Lords, and Attendants*

HENRY BOLINGBROKE
>Kind uncle York, the latest news we hear
>Is that the rebels have consumed with fire
>Our town of Cicester in Gloucestershire;
>But whether they be ta'en or slain we hear not.

Enter NORTHUMBERLAND

5 Welcome, my lord what is the news?

NORTHUMBERLAND
>First, to thy sacred state wish I all happiness.
>The next news is, I have to London sent
>The heads of Oxford, Salisbury, Blunt, and Kent.
>The manner of their taking may appear
10 At large discoursed in this paper here.

HENRY BOLINGBROKE
>We thank thee, gentle Percy, for thy pains;
>And to thy worth will add right worthy gains.

Enter LORD FITZWATER

LORD FITZWATER
>My lord, I have from Oxford sent to London
>The heads of Brocas and Sir Bennet Seely,
15 Two of the dangerous consorted traitors
>That sought at Oxford thy dire overthrow.

HENRY BOLINGBROKE
>Thy pains, Fitzwater, shall not be forgot.
>Right noble is thy merit, well I wot.

Enter HENRY PERCY, *and the* BISHOP OF CARLISLE

ACT 5, SCENE 6

Windsor Castle. Trumpets blow. HENRY BOLINGBROKE, DUKE
OF YORK, *and other lords and attendants enter.*

HENRY BOLINGBROKE

> Kind uncle York, the last news I heard is that the
> rebels have burned down the town of Cirencester in
> Gloucestershire. But I haven't heard if they've been
> captured or killed.

> NORTHUMBERLAND *enters.*

> Welcome, my lord. What's the news?

NORTHUMBERLAND

> First, I wish you happiness. Next, I've sent the heads
> of Oxford, Salisbury, Blunt, and Kent to London. This
> paper tells how they were taken.

HENRY BOLINGBROKE

> I thank you, gentle Percy, for your effort. I'll reward you
> well, as you deserve.

> LORD FITZWATER *enters.*

LORD FITZWATER

> My lord, I've sent the heads of Brocas and Sir Bennet
> Seely from Oxford to London. They were two of the
> traitors who wanted to overthrow you at Oxford.

HENRY BOLINGBROKE

> I won't forget your efforts, Fitzwater. I know that you
> deserve your noble title.

> HENRY PERCY *and the* BISHOP OF CARLISLE *enter.*

HENRY PERCY

> The grand conspirator, Abbot of Westminster,
> 20 With clog of conscience and sour melancholy
> Hath yielded up his body to the grave.
> But here is Carlisle living, to abide
> Thy kingly doom and sentence of his pride.

HENRY BOLINGBROKE

> Carlisle, this is your doom:
> 25 Choose out some secret place, some reverend room,
> More than thou hast, and with it joy thy life;
> So as thou livest in peace, die free from strife.
> For though mine enemy thou hast ever been,
> High sparks of honor in thee have I seen.

Enter **EXTON**, *with persons bearing a coffin*

EXTON

> 30 Great king, within this coffin I present
> Thy buried fear. Herein all breathless lies
> The mightiest of thy greatest enemies,
> Richard of Bordeaux, by me hither brought.

HENRY BOLINGBROKE

> Exton, I thank thee not; for thou hast wrought
> 35 A deed of slander with thy fatal hand
> Upon my head and all this famous land.

EXTON

> From your own mouth, my lord, did I this deed.

HENRY BOLINGBROKE

> They love not poison that do poison need,
> Nor do I thee. Though I did wish him dead,
> 40 I hate the murderer, love him murdered.
> The guilt of conscience take thou for thy labor,
> But neither my good word nor princely favor.
> With Cain go wander through shades of night,
> And never show thy head by day nor light.

HENRY PERCY

The Abbot of Westminster, who conspired against you, has died. But here is Carlisle, alive, to hear your judgment on him.

HENRY BOLINGBROKE

Carlisle, here is your sentence: pick some secret place where you can live out your life in peace and die without violence. Even though you've always been my enemy, I've seen that you are a man of great honor.

EXTON enters, with several people carrying a coffin.

EXTON

Great king, here is your greatest fear now buried inside this coffin. In it lies without breathing your greatest enemy, Richard of Bordeaux, brought here by me.

HENRY BOLINGBROKE

Exton, I don't thank you. By killing him, you've done a disgrace to my name and to our country.

EXTON

I did this on your own command.

HENRY BOLINGBROKE

Those who need to poison someone still don't love poison. Even though I wanted him dead, I hate the man who murdered him, and now I love the man who has been murdered. You can take your guilty conscience as payment. I won't give you any praise or royal favors. Go wander the night like **Cain**, and don't show your face here again.

In the Book of Genesis, Cain kills his brother, Abel, and, as punishment, God orders him to wander the earth for the rest of his life. Cain is considered the world's first murderer.

Exeunt **EXTON** *and his men*

45   Lords, I protest, my soul is full of woe
        That blood should sprinkle me to make me grow.
        Come, mourn with me for that I do lament,
        And put on sullen black incontinent.
        I'll make a voyage to the Holy Land,
50   To wash this blood off from my guilty hand.
        March sadly after. Grace my mournings here
        In weeping after this untimely bier.

Exeunt

EXTON *and his men exit.*

Lords, I protest. My soul is full of sorrow that blood
has been shed to make me more secure. Come, mourn
with me and dress yourselves in black immediately. I'll
travel to the Holy Land to wash away this blood from my
guilty hands. March sadly behind me, and weep for this
untimely death.

They exit.

Notes

Notes

Notes

Notes

Notes